HUMCA

House Work

House Work

A Novel By

Kristina McGrath

Bridge Works Publishing Company
Bridgehampton, New York

All rights reserved under International and Pan-American Copyright Conventions. Published 1994 in the United States by Bridge Works Publishing Co., Bridgehampton, New York. Distributed in the United States by National Book Network, Lanham, Maryland.

First Edition

Library of Congress Cataloging-in-Publication Data

McGrath, Kristina.
    House work : a novel / Kristina McGrath.—1st ed.
       p.   cm.
    ISBN 1-882593-07-3 (alk. paper)
    I. Title.
    PS3563.C3659H68   1994
    813'.54—dc20   94-13257
                                         CIP

10 9 8 7 6 5 4 3 2 1

Cover art by Kristina McGrath in the collection of Ann Watkins and Jim Calhoun. Used with permission.

Book and jacket design by Edith Allard

Printed in the United States of America

Because of my mother,
Eva Ann Frombach,
start of grace

Acknowledgments

With thanks to the editors of *The American Voice*, where the following chapters originally appeared in slightly different form: "Housework," "In the Quiet," "Our Father's Room," and a portion of "Hers." "Housework" was reprinted in *The Pushcart Prize, XIV*, in *Catholic Girls*, Penguin/NAL, and in *Love Stories For the Rest of Us*, an anthology from *The Pushcart Prize* series. An earlier version of "Life Before with Tumbledown Dad" was published in *Black Ice*. "Under the Table" appeared in *Catholic Girls and Boys*, Penguin/NAL. "What She Knew" appeared in *The Kenyon Review*. I also gratefully acknowledge the support of Wolf Pen Writers Colony, Kentucky Arts Council, and New York Foundation for the Arts.

Thanks also to Frederick Smock for his friendship and editorial help; to Katherine McGrath Lewis; to William McGrath; to Jerry E. Berg, in loving memory; to Elizabeth Wray, Nancy Jay Crumbine, and Barbara Bedway for their friendship through all the years of this book; to Malaga Baldi, my agent, for her care of this book; and to Barbara Phillips for her editorial suggestions.

And, finally, with gratitude for the love and conversation of women in whose presence grace took shape; with special thanks to Fredda Pearlson, years of devotion, who took in strangers of this story and gave them brilliant shelter; to Laurie Ridgeway, for our daily peace and beauty; and to Lucia Stanton White, for her fierce intelligence, constant readings, bounty of days and nights.

Contents

Contents

Dearests

The Family, Afterward

A Prologue of Her Place

The light of it was made of wood and leafy brick, of hillside steps and watered trees. The light of it was enormous. At the headwaters of the Ohio, the rivers made it so. The bright green valley and its constant rains, the glassworks and steelworks of its sky did it, the sheared hilltop coal, beds of iron ore glinting along the base of the Allegheny Mountains, screech of its trolleys on sparking grooves, loops of silver railtrack curving along both sides of three rivers, breaking ground to someplace else.

The light of it was gray or white or blue or green, changed by rain or smoke or childhood. It was more a feeling than a color. It was something she knew. It was how she felt, from a far-off place (born Louise, daughter of Anna), all things come back into being.

She was born to the Hallisseys, to Anna and Guy, born to her sister Helen, to her brother Eddy, born in 1950 to the upriver craneman's siren, almost in time for the 12 o'clock Angelus, born to a city of gray mansions and trolley takers, into the sound of its trains, with painted bridges striding in one step to concrete shores, with mills blazing over rivers, making what is sure and true seem ghostly in the hours on earth.

Why was it always raining and burning there in this rock-sure city? The rivers and mills had a weather of their own. Memory makes its own atmosphere.

The smallest puffs of smoke gathered, then dispersed in the great beyond of its sky. Smoke poured out like music from a horn,

ix

House Work

the angel of fog rose up from the body of hillside neighborhoods, from wet river highways, and Pittsburgh seemed forever beyond itself, spiraling upward, where she was born, a daughter to some, sister to others, a lover of sorts, the youngest of three, Lulie Hallissey kicking a nettle down the street.

Housework

Anna and Guy, 1945–1955

Housework

Anna

⚑ The world would come to an end, she thought, and ⚑ she'd be here hand-washing his linen handkerchiefs.

She loved the dangerous rush of water, the small white sink near brimful. There were at least ten things left to do before he got home, but she stood at the sink and listened, scrubbing the linen thin, taking pleasure in the way light fell through the cloth when she held each handkerchief to the fluorescent.

Anna Hallissey loved fluorescent light. Fluorescent never lies, she thought, and scrubbed the linen thin.

She loved to feed him. She honestly loved to clean his clothes. And when she picked up what he let fall to the floor, mended his underwear or just plain splurged and bought him new ones, she felt that she healed him, partook of him, and life also. What she touched, he ate, he wore, was where he sat or crossed space. The peeled peach (he insisted on it) was so ripe, so intimate, had been touched nearly everywhere, had changed shape even, that it almost embarrassed her to see him eating it with absolute faith.

She pictured him, and he sat there, Guy Hallissey, spotless and eating a peach. It was 1948. She was the secret of his magnificence, and the handkerchiefs rose higher with the water.

Not that she ever thought of it that way. It just made her feel good to have everything done for him. He was somebody. And, he could be so appreciative. Not that that was everything, or anything really. The doing was everything, and the thanks was just a little something extra. Well, yes, she decided almost guiltily, she liked to be thanked, it made it nice. She loved it when he knew exactly who he had married. Anna Evaline Jacob. Three years ago, come end of June.

You're so good for me, we'll give it a whirl, he said, get married, and she nearly keeled right over. As if God himself had come down from heaven just to tell her: What you are doing for me is fine.

She had said no to marriage more than once or twice. His was her fifth proposal. It seemed that every man and his brother from the North Side of Pittsburgh who was just a little too nice or too shy or too something, had wanted to marry her; but he was somebody. He did drink just a little too much. But she would make him a life so good, he would have no reason for running from things as they are. The regatta of his handkerchiefs floated in the sink.

4

Life is either pleasant or my responsibility to make it so, she thought. Another clean Monday. She shut the taps and slapped the sink. 100 percent linen, she said. He would be home soon.

With the car door slam, the songs began. He loved to make up little stories about his day at the Radiant Oven Company by stringing together various song titles and phrases. After roaring up to the curb, skidding on the cobblestone of Franklin Way, shutting off the motor and the radio songs, he boomed. Right then and there in front of the neighbors. Waving from their porches, they seemed to appreciate it, so she didn't mind enjoying it herself. He climbed the twenty-four steps of the rented house at 432 Franklin Way, one of many narrow alleyways cut from the backs of east-side streets, crowded with small high houses towering in tight rows near Trenton Avenue and the trolley line. The high house suited him. He waved back at the neighbors from the landing, and the door swung open.

Finding her there with everything dropped perfectly into place, including herself at the door, he'd widen his eyes and grin but keep on singing, and without the loss of one beat, hurl himself onto the sofa in time to *I've Got a Gal* (he sat) *in Kalamazoo* (he crossed his legs with a flourish). And she knew that must be Miss Glenny Hayes from Michigan, *Shoo Shoo Baby* (who had been fired), *My Darling, My Darling,* in *Tulip Time* (it was spring), *All Dressed Up in a Broken Heart* (he was sad to see her go). Then suddenly remembering her, he'd say, Whoops well so how are you? and then they'd laugh. He was the first

5

person in the world who had ever really spoken to her in such full sentences.

And so, with an old bent butter knife, she crawled to some far-off corner (he would be home soon) and began scraping the floorboards, unimportant, invisible really because of the monstrous furniture, except to her, she knew it was there. Dirt should be taken care of like the first small sign of sadness or flu. Otherwise, catching his eye, it would spread under the feet of their company, gad about like sugar, unfurl into the yards of lazy neighbors, the whole city a shambles before you knew it, if each one in it did not take it on under their own roof. Besides, he noticed everything.

It made him happy to see her doing things, and she was happy to be of use while listening to the radio news. The world interested her, but there was that problem with the newspaper, a year or yes it was two ago (it was his, he said, snatching it back), so she never touched it again. *She's Funny That Way,* he sang.

Things made such an impression, she thought, as she scraped behind the china closet, remembering that time as a schoolgirl in the convent she loved so much. She had accidentally stepped on a white chrysanthemum in the convent yard. It had fallen from some poor excuse for a bush that Sister What-was-her-name-anyway cared for, every day of her life it seemed she was out there, digging. She liked talking to nuns. Well not really talking, just listening to them pass in the halls, mouse mouse mouse and holy holy holy (she counted them) was enough. She was one of the chosen, sent regularly on errands, who got to see nuns actually do things like stir soup or crouch digging by a bush. She felt it under her foot. The old nun scowled and lifted, with thumb and forefinger, as if it were a repulsive thing, the tip of her old brown shoe that was always dancing in a place beyond itself. That, child, the old nun snarled, pointing at the chrysanthemum, could have been the heart of Jesus. Even now, eleven years later, she felt mortified. It could have been the old nun's heart itself, with all it had to live for other than that old bush. It could have been her own, or his. She promised to be more careful.

On those quick bird feet, on her small feet, she tiptoed on a Wednesday through the house when no one was there but her and her girl. She knew she was tiptoeing when the girl started it too. She stopped dead center on the cellar stairs on her way to the kitchen and set down her heels. Perhaps she had made a mistake, she thought, he was not the marrying kind. There was one child already; he loved little Helen Marie like the dickens, capable of it, with his enormous hugs and walks around the reservoir or up and down the alley all the time, always showing her off. And he loved Grandpap too; he sacrificed the corner bedroom so her dad would have a home. My dad is no trouble, he's as good as a mouse, she thought, he hardly says a word except to Guy, and the two of them go out together for a good time at the Palisades Cafe.

But what were these sudden outbursts, what had she done? (Everything around here has my name on it, he told her. First comes me.) Perhaps it was the eggs this morning that made him a stranger. At 6 A.M. when he was slamming through the fry pans, she went to an empty room, shut the door, and gave him time. She had broken the yolks. She had done something. She would sit there at the edge of the bed, half the morning if she had to, and find it out.

She set down her heels on the cellar stairs, her arms filled with sheets. Helen Marie, we're tiptoeing, she said, and pressing down lightly on her head, she set her girl flat on steady feet again, then scooted her into the late afternoon light that filled the yellow kitchen, where she seasoned a pot of water with a confident dash of salt.

She had the cookbooks memorized like Shakespeare plays. It was a common form of magic, pulling suppers from midair and boiling water on a low budget. Rattling something silver, at her business of which she was fond, of feeding who was hers and scooting them into a design around the table, she built with pots and pans the idyll of her mind, and this was daily life: around it with a rag, picking up after it, rowing with the oar of it to the Mother of God.

She ran up the stairs two at a time to the bedroom closet with an armful of sheets. The days were like rows of her bargain shoes that shone in the closet next to his, two-toned and Italian made. And here was the sound of the nineteenth century in a long dress brushing against the cold plaster as she pushed through the closet. So this was life and this was life. And there was the buff-colored cat on the roof, climbing toward some higher realm where things would work out.

Things would work out because she was in love with the everlasting furniture, with the restfulness of plates stacked in painted cupboards, with the raising of husbands and children all the way down the alley, because she knew she was a part of something that keeps so many alive.

She could please him, knowing the pleasure of safe mason jars and the calm of wooden spoons, the thud of good wood (her mother would have made that sound had she lived). Something sure as a cake could be done, and all of this was great and kind, small hellos to God. She would take care of hers, her corner of it would be a place to live.

Downstairs, cut carrots ran through water rolling in its pot. The silverware lay ordered in blue shoeboxes with cardboard partitions in the deep drawers with which they were blessed. He had painted flowers and she had painted leaves on the faces of drawers and cupboards, the two of them conspiring in some small but complicated plot against the larger tides of tornados and gunshots, of derelicts, senators and failed lovers, to be here, be counted, she said, in this strange world.

Good people, she reminded herself, are recorded in books. Everyone had at least one thing to be recorded. Any sadness you might have is often recorded as a good work. This is the way it is, she said to herself, in love with the beautiful ordeal of packing the sheets in the small upstairs closet. A good house, she thought, and slapped the sheets. Love, she said, this would sustain, and the feeling went with her into the supermarkets, into the streets, God bless us all. The feeling could go as far as the Radiant Oven Company, into the world, he would carry it there to Penn Avenue. And so she went on with it, this knowledge of where everything absolutely is, all the designs of which she was capable, as she built, to the last detail, the house from the inside.

And he had helped. His heart was to the wheel. He had given her a floor to match her Sunday dress. He painted it yellow with black polka dots, each dot a monument to something they could not understand. He loved doing and doing, yet how he sweated when he did it, sprawled there like a little boy or folded all upon himself, bug-eyed in the corner, goggling his own perfection for days afterward, visiting it like a relative, and they said it couldn't be done. But everything was possible, she thought, what a talent. And told him so. You are a talented man. Everything he did, floor, drawer, arabesques he sawed into tables and shelves, he ran to have her see, and she would say, How lovely. Tasks like this made him kind, and when he wasn't, well she had enough love to change ten people. He showed promise, able to love like that, a floor. She had the power. She was in the house.

She had joined history. She was in the house. I love how you touch things, he told her, I always know where to find them afterward. When she reordered the drawers, or plumped the sofa where he either burrowed or sprawled depending on his mood, it seemed to calm him.

Though sometimes it seemed he was beyond her like the congressmen and the senators, only a little nearer, when he screamed like that, questioning where she'd been, who had she been with. Everything was converging in their own bedroom, as if they were in an auto accident with history. My husband, right or wrong, she said, wishing there was someone to talk to about birth, about Hollywood and the attorney general, about Hoover, about hiccups. The child Helen still preferred crying to any other form of human expression. Mouse mouse mouse, she sang to the child. She was expecting again, and the house seemed to run under her feet. Two months pregnant, he screamed. Who were you with two months ago? But she would take care of everything. She knew how.

Housework made her dizzy sometimes, the way the seasons did when she thought of them too much, how they kept reoccurring like stacks of dirty dishes. She stood at the sink, washing the dishes, feeling at peace with the whiteness of the appliances. Eventually it was their youngest, their third child, their last, who would replace the seasons and the dishes as an image of time, where she saw herself as a part of some great wheel, where she was lost, important, found, small, and going on from there in a spin, but now it was mainly the dishes that made her feel eager, indebted.

Why, some of the best things in the world, she thought, happen like housework, in circles. Birth and death, for example, not that you could call that best. Funny, but it wasn't *anything* really, it was just *everything*, whole kit and caboodle, one of the few facts (people get born and they die) that was neither good nor bad, though secretly she was convinced: birth was good, death was bad; and she was here and so she swept, on the fifth day, the floor for the fifth time that week. (They hated sugar under their shoes, and he was always leaving it there.) And so she swept (the broom was new and

11

bristly) as she said her secret prayer for her father never to die.

Her actions, she felt for a moment, were like those of God. He repeated himself too, heaping snow and flowers, tornadoes and children down onto earth, taking them away, then heaping it all back down again. God was like one huge housewife, she thought, then blessed herself for the blasphemy. And please, she whispered into the towels, let it be a son.

Anyways, she thought, everything big was patterned after something small, even though they told her it was the other way around. She stuffed the towels into the washer, considering the idea. Neighborhood pride, for example. Why, all he had to do was put in one new step, let alone the whole set that he did, and there were new steps all the way down the block, a whole way of life born from a single set of steps. Enough good alleys like this and you'd have a city. I bring you, she said, this handkerchief, this man; this birdsong, symphony; this washed-down wall, this whole shebang. She was brimful with the idea of babies. This woman, she thought, and stopped.

This was silliness, and *skittery*, she said, liking the word better than what it meant. The insides of the washing machine twisted back and forth like the shoulders of someone at the scene of an accident. Her daughter made a sound, and suddenly she remembered the head of that lovely African insect she saw in *Life* last night. It resembled the monkey, and the monkey, man; though little girls, she thought, wiping her daughter's chin, resembled nothing and nobody but maybe other women. Your

12

Mummy's a real rumdum, a real odd bird, she said to her girl, making her laugh.

She was afraid to be such an odd brown bird. This was how she thought of herself when she thought too much. When she was in company, some party he was always dragging her to and then he never wanted to leave, she sat in a corner, seeking out other people (usually other women, and only with her eyes, she didn't want to start up anything like a conversation) who could possibly be odd brown birds, too. Actually, it wasn't odd at all. Brown birds are very common, she thought, except when you felt like one.

Just last night her husband screamed that there was something wrong with her. She felt (whenever he swore like that) picked up and thrown into herself. It just took a while to get back out again, that's all. Anyways, Tip tip, she said to her girl, taking her hand and climbing from the bottoms of the house, and thinking (that's what her daughter called it, the bottoms) there was probably some truth to what he said, because she did think too much.

She knew she thought too much when she found herself disagreeing with the Bible. Suddenly, at the top of the cellar stairs, she believed in evolution and hoped no one would ever find out. Who was she to disagree? Well, she must be somebody (she laughed and snapped the cellar light), because she did disagree, even with Darwin just a little, even if it was as a little joke. Man, she agreed, descended from the monkey—already her son, not yet born or of any shape much beyond light inside her, scrambled like one and tasted bittersweet and sure as mud, while her daughter, born, sat there, like an unborn,

13

like a piece of silk—and women (she went on) descended from space itself (outer space), resembling more a swirl of air than anything with a nose on it.

She meant no disrespect. Women were strangers, unfamiliar in their babushkas, their getups, odd and poking in their heads with apology, waiting on their pins and needles to say hello. They apologized for a lack of salt in things they brought, for unrisen cakes, the rain, a husband's lack of social grace. They apologized for being happy (they were never happy, just a little flushed), sad (they were never sad, only slightly under the weather or a little light-headed), or there at all. Chafing at the bit, skirting the furniture, or wringing their hands in front of movie houses, they waited to be invited in and seated. Even in their own houses they were visitors, choosing wooden chairs. And when something buzzed, thudded, was still, they sprang into place, which was nowhere. Wherever they were, it was only temporary (they sat on window ledges, they stood on ladders). And finally, they weren't even sure about being pedestrians in public spaces. She watched from windows their feet brimming over curbs or onto them (they raced on their toes), letting automobiles or businessmen pass. They looked funny through the glass, distorted somehow (and pity-full, she said) like large girls.

Men were such a relief. And she was here, sure-footed, taking care of one. She enjoyed it. Being inside the house was a comfort. She felt sorry he couldn't get to be a woman, too, sometimes. Large spaces made her anxious lately, especially when she thought of how she used to cross them, on horseback no less, at a gallop.

Even now it made her giddy. Silenced at the moment of the jump, she soared (or rather the old moment did) inside her body, and from this great height she looked down on it (her body), a stranger with whom she no longer liked to dance. Lately she never got far into conversation or Lake Erie, except a toe. A seashell was ocean enough for her and she'd let him do the talking. She rocked her girl.

He was on this talking jag. All a lot of me me me or about people's rumps, everything flowered with parts of the body. You may as well listen to nothing as to that. He was drinking too much, flirting with anything in a skirt, and what was worse, he spit on people's porches. (He was getting out of hand—and then he bought her flowers.) It was just another of his many jokes as they stood there marooned on the porch. Thank God, the nice people (relatives) hadn't answered the door yet. Giving him one of her famous looks (at his feet), she bent down and with her new white handkerchief (the one with her maiden initials stitched on it, she loved her own name), wiped at the bleached porch boards, and with the opening door, rose up and smiled.

Housework, she thought, was an act of forgiveness for what you read in the newspaper. (He no longer minded that she read it; he was always off somewhere she didn't name.) By having supper always on time, whether he showed up or not, she felt she forgave some great evil, or death itself, by the fact she went on with it.

The girl in her lap was laughing now and talking of ponies, ready to play alone again. She always invited Helen everywhere through the house, if she cared to come, though lately she did not. The child shook her head to the outstretched hand, preferring not to go into the kitchen (she dropped greens into water, flooded a pot in a rush of metal at the sink), into the cellar (she swept with a sawed-off broom the last of black water into the bubbling holes of the floor drain), into the upstairs room (she set out his clothes for the evening, he appreciated it). The girl was forever plopping herself down and having to jump back up again this time of day, late late afternoon (her mother tempted her along with songs) until she gave it up and sat, smack down on the floor in the middle of the hallway. Little white ponies, baby ones, she said to her girl and, racing by, tickled her on the stomach with her mouth, then was off again on her toes in the staccato of last-minute tasks. What was mean or ugly was not going to stop her, she swore it, from finding something to look forward to.

Her son was born. Edward Patrick Hallissey. She could hardly bear to look at him she loved him so much. Real corn, she thought, but that's the way I am. She felt accomplished as she climbed down the cellar stairs with her son in a basket. It was 1949.

She felt so clear and sad about the world when she did laundry. She liked this feeling of melancholy. It made her feel like she was telling the truth. It made her feel large, and above her head (she saw it), her soul seemed to drift like a paper boat out the cellar window into the gray sea of all Pittsburgh.

Cellar light was like a trapped thing and the same in every house. She studied it on walks. Windows half above, half below ground interested her, and the tops of ladies' heads bobbing in an element like water at twilight. It was always twilight in cellars, even in summer, even at noon. Down there the day was always ending like someone good who was dying. It made her want to stop and talk on her walks to the store. She imagined herself kneeling at cellar windows, Hey, and tapping on the glass, Hello, all the way down the block. The ladies would be shocked. What a novelty. Seeing someone there full in the face. Not the usual detachments: sawed-off ankles and shoes, the eerie crawl of living hoses and grass overhead, all things plain, misunderstood into wonderment or fear, or found there as they truly were, a wonderment, a fear: the earth was there, it was watered, it was soft, though sliced, suspended over your head, a lid; the living ones walked there in their shoes, their feet ran to meet each other. But here, a sudden human face, flesh, eyes. From sheer surprise, the ladies' heads would rise like balloons into daylight, followed shortly after by their bodies, one by one, ascending into Wilkinsburg (their skin and dresses would be damp, smelling of soap, storage, and earth, the twilight smell of warm leftover water, of green things kept out of light, also the sweetness of their tied-back hair) and, bursting into view, bumping into one another, all twenty-three of them at once, they would chat, the women of Franklin Way, east side of Pittsburgh.

Dazzling, she thought. And in a rare backward look: I would have been a poet were it not for Sister What-was-her-name. She kissed six of her son's ten perfect fingers in time to the beat of Sister What-was-her-name, six

17

kisses springing from the invisible rhythms of her invisible thought. She should have been a poet, she thought, because she felt aware of things that other people forgot. Not many took pride in what they did. But what she did made her sing, high and slow, this melancholy (so long as it didn't go on about itself more than it had to—she hated anybody brooding) made her feel like she loved her own heart. Always she had this slightest inkling she was somebody.

She held his head for hours and listened. He was so easily upset. President Truman recently told her that the Russians had set off an atomic explosion, and she wished he wouldn't find out. And not about this morning sickness either. He was still upset about that Alger Hiss and his Communist spy ring, so they said. Gospel truth, sons a bitches, he said, We'll be on their plates in the end. He sat on the sofa, with his legs crossed, flipping his ankle.

Helen Keller was on the radio last night, she said, ironing, wanting to tell him something nice. Helen Keller listens to the radio, donya know. So how does she do it? Well, it seems she can just feel it. Sound has vibrations, you know, and all she has to do is touch the radio and there it is, the song. He nodded, and slept.

It would be such a joy, she thought, gliding the iron across the deep green of his work shirt, to see Miss Helen Keller actually listening to music. A true and happy Christian, Miss Keller sways lightly by the radio. It was an act of grace to find something lovely. Helen Keller waves a hand to the rhythms of "Tuxedo Junction," and with the other listens. In Helen's house everything has to be just so, they said, otherwise walking across the room would be a terrible danger, from the stairs to her study, a terrible risk. It's like you're in the right church, but which pew do you go into? Was it like stepping through her own mind? she wondered. "Miss Keller rises early and answers all her own letters." The announcer's voice sounded almost merry.

No one was ungrateful for Helen's sorrow. Everyone seemed to believe in it so, as if Jesus himself lay across her eyes and ears. After all, exactly who would Helen be without her sorrow? To what do you attribute your success? asked no one. Our little agonies, your gifts, she answered the same no one, and stared at his body, slumped and snoring.

Any day now she would have to tell him. She was pregnant with their third child. He was still in the middle of his fuss about the boy, and she couldn't scrape up the nerve; it would be like the newspaper, it would be like the eggs, he'd lose his head. The doctor told her she was in no condition to have two children right in a row, what with the miscarriages she had had so far. Her head reeled, but the start of the child pulled her to earth with its own slight gravity. She had told her sister weeks ago. You're thin as a rail, sick as a dog, her sister said, and hit the roof; You have no business being pregnant. We will all come out of this better people, she thought; it was a sin to be unhappy.

It was that old public high school feeling. It was a standing joke at Schenley High: Doncha get it, she's Catholic; and the iron shimmied in small tight strokes on the collar of his Richmond Brothers shirt. She stood off in the distance again, it was 1941 in the public school yard

19

by a wire fence. She shuffled her feet, burrowing into the dirt with the tip of her shoe, her own slight place. She watched the others run shouting across the yard, their sound lost now, but their bodies still twisting with laughter eight years later as if poked with invisible sticks. She stared at the crowd of young men and women. They could all be sent off to war or marriage, packed into houses or trenches, with bad grammar and (she gave them the benefit of the doubt) the tenderness of their pin-cushion hearts. You're nothing, she thought, without your sorrow. She wished they would all stop having such a good time. Germany was the place of her birth and the den of devils. It was 1941 by a wire fence in America, and it was a sin to be unhappy. For lack of money she had to be sent to Schenley High and there went peace and quiet, the convent, the singing lessons. (Not that she'd ever wanted to be a nun, she didn't, she loved horses, children, tennis, men.) That was the only thing she had ever pleaded for, those singing lessons, and now, without them, she saw all the little *O* mouths of the people, empty and soundless, and his, opening and closing. Without your little sorrows, she knew it, you saw nothing beyond your own nose. She made an *O* in the flowered rug with the tip of her shoe. She looked at it and it made her like everyone a little more.

Housework had a rhythm like prayer. During a Hail Mary, God help him, the iron wobbled over the difficult cloth of his work pants and snagged, burnishing and polishing at the slightest touch. He hated that, the burnt shine on his trousers or shirt pockets. God help Guy Hallissey to be happy and nice, she said. Her stomach

20

felt wooden, but it made her real. Her legs felt flimsy, as if they were scribbled there in chalk beneath her, somewhere over the flowered carpet. Things would get better, life would improve. Imagine, she thought, something nice.

Imagine a tree in full blossom, she thought, a sunrise, a saint at your front door, begonias or snow on the sill outside your window and you refused to look. You missed out on something brief that would boost you and your husband and your children up forever. The sunrise, to her way of thinking, was a saint. She would have made a good pagan. There would be so many things to adore.

I should have been a pagan, she said to herself a few years later, and began a rosary then for Senator McCarthy to remain silent, to please shut his trap, as she caught her hand in the wringer and screamed—though it was nothing really, it was only for a moment, it was just the slightest thing.

Sitting on the Sofa

Guy

◫ Guy Hallissey sat on the sofa with his legs ◫ crossed, flipping his ankle, wishing he could shut up or fly and be rid of it one way or the other. Every time he opened his goddamned trap, he thought, he ruined everything.

He would sit here on the sofa and not say a single word, not one. Not about Moscow, Alger Hiss, or the man next door, not one about anything. And not a single wasted breath for the U.S. Navy, not ever again, he swore it.

He felt kicked out of the house of a relative or out of his life as a man when the Navy discharged him. That was six years ago, in 1943, and still he hated to sit and wait while the world went on around him.

He had been so excited to go.

He could feel himself in rare form, bouncing off the walls, reeling out the door, Guy Hallissey on his way to the Pacific or for a little spin around the block in November cold, but he sat on the sofa.

It was always like that. He would be sitting there feeling his oats, longing for the road, to be his own boy, with no one scolding him, no one frowning at him, and then she would do something like clang the pot, salt the soup, and he would stay on, his body suddenly weighted to the sofa, with his mind still trailing out the door.

Anna stood ironing by the window. No matter how much he praised the soup, she wouldn't smile. He must have said something terrible to her just the day before. He had an inkling, something about the man next door again, though he couldn't remember exactly what it was. But at the last word of it (whatever it was), in his mind he was buying flowers and she was feeling better.

The heat of the iron rose up around him with the bitter clean smell of the clothes dipped in a bucket of starch. She always did it that way, he knew it, he watched her once, he crouched on the stairs.

She used a metal bucket, it was silver, it was almost white. She filled it with water and a cup of powdered starch from a green and white box, soaked the clothes for ten minutes, hem-hawed around the cellar as they soaked (sweeping water with a too-small broom, wiping at windows too high above her head—she was always doing something), then wrung each piece out to dry, hanging each piece just so on the cellar line. She made the whole house reek of starch, and the clothes chilled him where he hid on the stairs, watching. Whenever she ironed the

23

clothes, still damp with the solution, the smell spread through the house, clinging to his eyes.

Cellar air, dark and wintry, spidered up from the floor vents into his sleeves and hair. He preferred summer, when the cold starched clothes, rolled tight in a zippered bag and chilled in the icebox, were a relief, when light and the day's heat lasted into evening, and when the next-door neighbors, the only ones on the block with a new Philco, would haul out the television set to a small patch of front lawn for everyone to watch *Texaco Star Theatre* with Milton Berle, or something once in a lifetime like the Schmeling fight, right there in front of your face, in summer air. He closed his eyes. Toss me down some heaven, he prayed, give me back some June.

He was ecstatic in summer, he refused to be still. He had a passion for water and he liked to take off to Lake Erie at any chance, grab his little girl Helen and teach her something essential about water and fun. He drove the highways one-handed at top speed, in perfect control, with an elbow out the window, with his starched sleeves rolled, and through the city he swerved to take the bumps, slamming the bumper to the concrete for her pleasure; he didn't care. Rolly coasters, she screamed, it made her laugh.

The lake was a copy of something he longed for in his mind. The touch of water, its thick brown silk. Its density upheld him and his affection, he could exhaust himself and float, he was alone on the planet, he could tire and he was soothed; and what he imagined was actual, there was a power like his own, there was a traveler like himself, there was something he knew, an opening, a rebellion against form, against his own tiny pickiness at lint, his critical assumptions, against his own fierce aim at himself; there was water, forgiveness and mercy, a beautiful dancer like himself, no resistance; there was water, a chance, a second soul; a big time, and he would plop his girl down in the middle of it; here's what we know of it: Lake Erie.

No need for cellars in summer. His wife used the line in the yard, and raised it high with the new aluminum clothes props he bought for her. He liked coming home to find the yard brimful with clothes snapped by the wind, waving white and mint green through the air. He liked to sit out there with the clothes for a while before supper. His little girl came out with him.

Helen Marie Hallissey was the pinkest of all girls possible with her golden hair. It was hard for him to believe he had anything to do with her being here in the first place. Sometimes, just to make sure, he pinched her nose. He always bent down to talk to her. Little stinker, he said, Little Helie, and pinched her cheek. He couldn't take his eyes from her as he watched her run, slapping through the long white sheets on the line, in and out of light, out of her mind with summer and the brightness of it all.

Iridescent gold and green in the evening near supper, nasty and almost dead, but humming around their heads, the flies flew at the chips of green paint at the back screen door, always ajar in summer. He would sit out there in his bleached T-shirt on the small back porch, going over his day, smoothing it down, drinking his Silver

Top beer, high above the yard with the laundry, until she called him in for supper. He would sit there planning a better door, a stronger porch, planning grass that was green at long last. He would concentrate hard against the clanging of pots, the rush of water at the sink, and his son's gurgling noises which seemed far off, unfamiliar like the distant motor of a stranger's car in the neighborhood.

The boy didn't look like him at all, he told her that all along. She was always doting over him, and he could see them at the side of his eye through the screen door. He had forgotten the flowers again, but he'd get her a new icebox just for a lark someday soon, a new yard, a decent porch, a whitewashed cellar.

Stranded high above the yard, feeling far from supper, he closed his eyes and thought of the cellar. The cellar was dark. Its walls were crumbly like ancient bread; they speckled his face with their spidery dust, with some terrible Communion, at the slightest touch. But then just a little shake, she rattled the dishes and brought him back. She lifted a lid, and the sound of it clanging back to its pot pleased him, along with the smell of boiled beef and carrots.

She's so good, he thought, what a living doll, and he really did adore her. She was a wonderful cook and he would tell her so. (You're a good little cook; I love this soup.) The broth would be thin and oily, too boiling hot for summer but blushed through with tomatoes, chock-full of meat and potatoes. He loved her soups, her too in his way. I love you in my own special way, he told her that often enough, knowing he had failed her, knowing he was just bouncing along, singing out of tune, full of his old malarkey.

The man next door (he opened his eyes; he could see him now through the window) seemed smug in his kitchen, pushing plates right and left with his elbows. He was just waiting for him to catch hell any second now from his wife. Listen, Buster, she'd say, I know what you've been up to. But the whole neighborhood, silent at its dinner, with newly whitewashed cellars below their feet (he knew it, if only he could see it), seemed satisfied and dumped into place, not about to budge one inch or ask one question in this heat. What have you been up to?

But no matter what was true, he would sit here, concentrate hard and figure whitewash, grass, new wood. And all the while the back porch sat high above the ground, shouldered against the breeze, like someone proud who was out of money. The steps sagged, weathered gray, their wood softened from too much Pittsburgh winter.

The steps were his own fault, he knew that. Fussy and wrecked after a long day of filling the rods with sand in the assembly line at the Radiant Oven Company, doing exactly what they told him to do, still he had his own commands: Each day was to be the cutting of an arabesque in wood, perfectly or else.

The rods were straight and hollow. There was a certain feeling, pin neat and pleasant, when he heard them snap into their clamps. He pulled the lever of the filling machine, which released the sand and started the motor. The rods vibrated, sure and humming, and the sand sifted down tight, buzzing through the pipes. He understood everything; it was perfectly clear. He taught her how salt and flour, pepper or sugar would settle in their tins if you slapped the bottom, preserving sacred space, and she was grateful. (She liked saving space, he knew it. They felt the same way.) He slipped in the pins at the top and bottom of the rods. When she worked there at the Radiant Oven Company during the war before they were married, she would spot weld the tips of the rods he had filled. They were in this together. The sand was baked into porcelain, the flour into cakes through some mystery of heat that was not his kingdom, somewhere down the assembly line where he could not see. The rods were bent into coils for electric stoves, and dark cakes suddenly appeared, frosted white, at the end of day. Life was a system and he had it down. He was his own boy, he was somebody, a big wheel in a paper hat. He pulled the lever, his feet planted firm, and he sang from absolute knowledge of this machine, from perfect boredom at every in and out, feeling grim and determined but singing all the while, nearly all eight hours of it each day, to waylay the feeling.

He knew the grass would never do. Pig-shit Irish, he said to himself, looking down at it from the porch. This yard was pig-shit Irish, something that his own drunken fool of a father would have let slip, tossed off to a gamble with the weather.

And now, near winter, with the idea of grass abandoned, he stayed inside, watching her. It was all he could do to stay put with his feet on the floor, stepping on the tail of his own dream. He needed a new garage, a whiter cellar, grass that was green. He would get the dough, he would see some guy about a horse. He had a few deals in the wind (Sink or swim, he told himself, and quit your hem-hawing around the house) but he sat stranded on the sofa, smoking two cigarettes at a time, drinking his coffee (with just a touch of Seagram's 7) from a thick white cup, and dunking his cake.

He watched Anna iron. The lamplight beside her made an island of her body with the pale white moon of her face floating above it. The light made a place for her, and she stood there, her body bright and hazy, the vene-tians behind her slatted dark with night. Her dress was faded yellow; its color clung to his eyes and made them close. Helen slept in the room upstairs just above his head, snug in her place with knees curled nearly to her chin, and when he closed his eyes, he saw her there under blue ticking, and her sleep was his own.

But then he knew, he remembered. He needed a new garage. He checked from the window. His car was still there, a brand-new '49 Plymouth. The old garage on Trenton Avenue wasn't safe enough, so he let it go. He closed his eyes against the arrival of the hard Pittsburgh snows, the chilled metal, a stolen antenna, the frozen windshield, the spot on the chrome below the sideview mirror, and he knew it, he needed a new garage.

In a sudden flicker of old movies, Anna snapped his white shirt out into air, catching sight at the far side of his eye, drawing him out as if to sea. His elbow landed in his lap. He was losing his balance even as he sat.

Lamplight was a lovely thing, he thought, at least when you watched it from the streets. But now as it traveled in tight busy circles speckled with a snow of dust over the lamps, it made him swim. He could hear the furnace churning out from the cellar, and the whole house seemed to turn on its wheel. It was the start of winter. It was the start of his shirt. His clothes were a heap in a wicker basket, they were nothing, they were formless and cold, until she got ahold of them and made them what they were: his clothes. He felt a blast of gratitude. The furnace hesitated; the house held still. Spread tight on the board, his shirt was becoming his shirt. Her hands were pink as she smoothed it, as the iron smoothed it, bearing down. He knew that if he touched her hands, they would be hot like the iron, and the feel of her skin made him jittery sometimes.

He jumped up, slammed the front door and went outside to touch the amber glass Indian on the hood of the Plymouth. It crouched there, sleek and cool. He would rest inside a while where the upholstery smelled of sports supplies. He turned on the motor just so the Indian would light up, and it did, in the dark, like some part of himself that no one saw. He bought it special, self-installed. Same for those decals of naked women on the dash—good-lookers with wavy red hair—not naked at all, she just called them that because they looked the part. She threatened to come out at midnight and scrape them off. He liked to check that they were still there. They were still there.

He peered over the wheel, eyed for absolute sure a long light strand of woman's hair on the dashboard. Somebody had put it there. Somebody up to no good. And this just to put him at the scene of a tragedy. Someone from the Catholic Church would find it out. It glinted like the tiniest of weapons against him. Nothing he hated worse than a lost hair, all the devil's according to him. It made him choke. Maybe he could risk it, tell her about it and she'd be rid of it for him. It had been floating through the city and on the currents of speed he had picked it up and that was that. He was not responsible, it meant no harm; she would tell him so, and he would be less lonely.

To Anna, the nicest and best girl I have ever known, someday he'd tell her that on a card. No one wants to hurt you, he said to himself. He shut off the motor (the Indian blinked) and he went inside, running to where he would hear something nice.

Helen Keller was on the radio last night, she said, ironing. She hadn't even noticed he was missing; good, he thought. She had her own dreams as she stood there ironing. He liked it when she thought too much and he could be invisible. Helen Keller listens to music, she said. He burrowed down into the sofa as if into her voice, where he could disappear. The small church of her story, he slipped inside. Because sound has vibrations, you know, she can just feel it.

Whenever she spoke, it was like the machines at the Radiant Oven Company, their hum and blur filling the rods with sand. She's so good, he thought. And listened or half listened. Let her believe what she needs to, it didn't matter. So long as she made some kind of sound where he could live, he would sit here and be a better man.

Looking Back

Anna

◧ She would stand here ironing forever. It calmed ◧
her. He wasn't always happy. She knew that.

It was June of 1950. He was useless, he said, he
should be in Korea.

The creak of the board, the confident slam of the
iron in its metal plate, it calmed her. With a breeze now
and then through the kitchen door. It circled the yard,
skittering leaves, and made sunlight shimmer and curl
through the screen.

Louise Katherine Anne Hallissey, their third and
last, had just been born two months ago, too little, she
thought, for such a long name (there were too many aunts
and cousins to please), but my little Lulie, she decided,
when the sunlight curled.

These months he could not sleep but woke up sweating in the middle of the night and wept at the edge of the bed in the room where the five of them slept.

He needed help. It had dawned on her like the unborn child. But the U.S. Navy, who knew him first, had known it all along.

He had been so excited to go. She remembered him exactly, in a place too filled with light, striding off like Sinatra with that 100 percent camel hair coat slung over his shoulder, saying good-bye to anyone available in the lunchroom of the Radiant Oven Company (including her, she worked there as a welder). Off to the Navy, he said; it was 1943. Then there he was, like a shot dog, back at work in six weeks with a medical discharge. Because of my bad heart, he said.

Guy Hallissey was nearly the only man there. She felt so sorry. But after all, your heart is not your fault. We'll take care of it, she said.

She hardly knew him then. But he always made such a fuss, she couldn't help but notice. The girls at Radiant Oven all liked him. They were all after him in fact, she could tell. She decided right then and there, in the employee lunchroom of the Radiant Oven Company on Penn Avenue, east side of Pittsburgh. He was somebody.

He was a clean man with a good head of hair that lay back from his forehead in thick dark waves. With his dark eyes and long eyelashes that curled up perfectly, funny, but she thought him pretty, even in his paper hat, or with starched collar and cuffs, in pinstripes and pin dots, with a touch of paisley. He should be in the woods, she thought, like a flower or a tree. After work at 5:10, the way his trousers swayed in the parking-lot wind reminded her of cattails. Even when he walked, he danced.

She studied his large steps across cement sparkled with chips of sunlight. He was jingling the coins in his pocket, he was singing through his teeth. His shoes, two-toned and wing-tipped, always looked like he bought them yesterday. With lanky grace, the whole of him swung; yes, it was exactly like that, she was sure of it, the beauty of cattails. And now, seven years later, she liked to think of him that way, in the asylum of his beautiful shoes, in the refuge of his perfect appearance, dressed by angels, his tailors blameless.

He arranged his pale white hands, bumpy with good blue veins, his wrists and forearms stemming perfectly from rolled cuffs; at delicate angles they rested on tables and gave her the impression of strength and the fussiness of flowers all at once. He was a medium man, not tall or short, his fingers not stubby or long, his hair not black but not brown, his voice not worthy of song but you couldn't wait to hear what he would sing next. She was glad that his nose was the slightest bit paunchy, otherwise it would be too beautiful to bear, coming upon him suddenly in the fluorescent lunch room.

She worked there at the oven company in the third-floor Cartridge Department after a time at the downtown B & G Restaurant. Straight out of high school, in anklets and saddle shoes, with a ribbon in her hair, she remembered herself as she stood there ironing. Nightly, she polished her shoes and hung washed ribbons on a hanger by the window. She was fussy about herself, worried at

34

being a little too plump, serving liverwurst to business-men. She was happy when they ordered liverwurst. It was one of her favorite words at the time. She loved the loop of her own letters on the food checks. She loved the *l* in liverwurst. And "lettuce" she wrote, just to please her-self; she liked to spell things out, even when she was in a hurry. They wanted her to stay and told her so; little Anna Evaly, they called her; people seemed to eat more when she was around. But she knew you couldn't stay at the B & G forever.

The Radiant Oven Company suited her. She could improve herself, the way her aunts said she should. She started out in typing, but her boss had roving hands. She applied for a transfer out to the floor; she had her reasons, she said. Wearing her hair in a snood (which always bothered her, she had such a nice head of hair, it was a shame to waste it in a snood), and wearing the best of trousers from Standard Pants Men's Store on Fourth Ave-nue, where she bought all her pants and shirts, she felt happily employed, making the tiniest of tubes and baffles for curling irons and percolators, while two floors above her, he made the heating coils for electric stoves, until the war turned it all into welding. Later, she packed the heating units for submarines in crates so large she liked to joke that if she had fallen in, she could have easily ended up on a submarine.

He came back from his six weeks in the Navy. His songs were slow and melancholy as if he had fallen down piano keys into the lower notes. She looked after him from then on, making sure the others didn't get too close.

Isn't she pretty? He was always saying that, pulling

35

her down to his lap in the lunchroom at work, or in front of the aunts who raised her, her Duntes Fritz and Simmons who didn't approve. My Little Princess, he wrote on a card, for no reason but that it was spring. He was a wonderful man.

By '45, she knew it, she wanted a home. And if it couldn't be with him, then it wasn't going to be with anyone.

They married in June of 1945. She had to leave the Radiant Oven Company then; no married women allowed. She didn't like the policy but who was she to say so; she wanted a home.

Five years of marriage, she said to herself as she stood there ironing. Five years of marriage and three whole kids, she said. This was her first month up out of bed and around the house again since she gave birth to the girl by cesarean section. Never again, the doctor told her. She had been down with pneumonia since the girl was born, and the doctor said she had nearly died, but she wasn't going to believe that. Lulie Hallissey was too small to kill a flea.

Lately, every day, midafternoon when the kids were asleep at their nap and she counted them in her head, one two three, assuring herself they were there under the colors of their blankets, white blue pink, she sat in his chair and read the obituaries, prayed for the two miscarriages she had had so far, and prayed for the names of strangers there. But for the grace of God, she thought, every last one of them could have meant something to me.

As she stood there ironing she suddenly saw herself

sitting there reading the obituaries, half expecting to find his name, and it was settled now in her mind. There was something wrong. There had been all along.

Right before Lulie was born she sat with him on the cellar stairs, holding his hand. He would not stop talking about Senator McCarthy and the nuclear bomb, World War III and the Reds, his voice ambitious, taking on an era. He sounded just like the radio, she thought. There was a plot, he said. It had reached Pittsburgh, their very own neighborhood, right here in Wilkinsburg. It was in their house, all the way from Washington.

It had reached the Radiant Oven Company. The men at work threw pennies from the fifth-floor window, he told her when she found him crouched on the stairs in the darkness. They had him by the shoulder. He had to stand at the window and watch the pennies, there were five of them, little orange specks, fall through the air and land, scattering like a tiny explosion on the lot below. She could see it in her mind. An explosion, he said. Jump, they told him. He almost did. Go get them, go fetch them, fly.

The cellar steps were damp underneath them and she worried for him, that he might be chilled. No one wants to hurt you, she told him. Just to make sure, she would take a trolley to the Radiant Oven Company first thing the next morning and ask them straight out, What are you doing to my husband?

He saw things; she knew it, but it was hard to keep track of what was true and what was his head or his liquor. In a plain room (she imagined it then in her mind

37

with its tight beds tucked flat like small white prairies), hers was the light coming in from the window but his were the shapes it took. The bedroom bureau, its shadow, its big-shouldered defiance, its rounded face and grinning drawers, he said it frightened him on nights he could not sleep. The curtain hid a stranger. At times it was her. One minute she was a lovely cook, such a good little mother, the nicest girl he ever knew, and the next, well, she wouldn't repeat it. Whenever he screamed like that, accusing her of some nonsense (he knew what she was up to), she would remind herself he saw things, he wasn't always nice.

We'll get you some help, then you'll be fine. She was certain of it then as she sat with him on the stairs, he wasn't always well. With his knees to his chest, with one dusty shoulder huddled against the whitewashed wall. The cellar drafts blew upward from the damp into their sleeves and hair, and she whispered into the palm of his hand. I'll take care of it, she said. Then you'll be fine, then we'll be happy; it will be like before.

Though years ago and right from the start, there was reason enough to go straight to his mother. There's something wrong with him, she said. There's nothing wrong with my son except you. He's told us plenty for us to know that.

She felt foolish coming back alone from the Radiant Oven Company that day. There's nothing wrong with your husband, they told her, He's pulling your leg. What a joker, they said, He's full of malarkey. But it had already dawned on her like the unborn child. And though he wouldn't hear of it, he needed help.

*　　*　　*

38

There was something wrong. It was April of 1950. They had just finished supper and she said it was time, she was calling her sister and a taxi, and he agreed, My head hurts me. The doctor told me I could pick any day this week, she told him. It was a matter of lesions, loss of function, the doctor said so, Pick any day this week, that baby has got to come out.

She felt flimsy, of no weight, standing somewhere right above the sidewalk in front of the house. She was the head of a single pin. She flagged down the taximan who laughed, Well you sure don't look pregnant; and her husband just stood there. She touched his sleeve. It's time, she said. But he wouldn't get into the taxi. There's something wrong with my head, he told her. And the taximan snapped, Listen, Mister, in or out. Then off he walked in his own direction, To submit myself, he said.

He had rattled the door, she was still hanging out of it, and it swung now on its hinges. The baby turned in circles. Any minute she was going to ruin this taxi. She slammed the door. The taxi jolted forward and sped off down Franklin Way through a stop sign.

The taximan checked on her through the rearview mirror. She was all jutted-out face and hips, palms flat on the seat. She looked back through the rear window of the cab and he was running now, the air filling up the back of his perfect white shirt. Round and clean, he floated off. She imagined herself having one last feeling. She decided she would have it for him.

Their third child was born. The baby was in a glass box, two months premature. Helen and Eddy had been packed

39

off in a rush to her sister's place, so she convinced her hospital to let her go. I'll have help, be perfectly fine, she told the doctor. My sister's right here; she's waiting for me in the car.

She took the 94 Morningside to her sister's place. Sick as a dog, said her sister, Why would they let you loose on the streets like this, let me keep the kids a while longer. Just one more hour, she told her, and went straight to him.

There he was all rumpled at St. Anthony's, under sedation, telling her he was not coming home (The man next door wants to kill me when I say hello), telling her the Navy would help, not him, he couldn't anymore.

So there she was in a downtown office, to no good purpose, to ask for money (against her grain and never again, she swore it). The U.S. Navy had something on a card. The card was yellow; the clerk wasn't looking. Psychosis-neurosis, or something, said the card, dated 1943. And, Dear God, she thought, reading it upside down, what was that? What did it mean? Had it been going on that long? She had married it. And why, she wanted to ask the U.S. Navy, had she spent all these years figuring out what they already knew. There was something wrong.

St. Anthony Hospital in Bloomfield had done him some good. (I'm not going to that doctor anymore, he said, He burnt me.) Schizophrenic behavior, they had told her, and she nearly keeled right over. But she had signed their paper, it would be a big help to him, they told her so.

He was calm then; there were moments. He was in

and out of light like a stitch. But the night sweats returned, and by summer, he was certain of it. She was no longer a suitable wife.

And for your information, he told her last night on his way out the door to the Palisades Cafe, there's something wrong with you, start packing, I'm keeping the kids.

There were moments all along when they both understood there was something (What alotta hooey) beyond him (Get away from me) that was in need of her (You're nothing), that would accept her assistance. Back and forth like the slap of sheets in the back of the house, Help me, I'm fine, he said, Gangway, You're seeing things.

She stood there ironing. Get out and go, she couldn't remember how many times he said that to her. Go ahead and leave, he told her, You'll never leave me. And she knew it was true. She was staying on. My husband right or wrong. No matter what, she said.

There were begonias on the windowsill, turned this way and that toward light, toward the sky over Pittsburgh, toward the fluorescent in the yellow kitchen. She could manage it, she thought as she stood there ironing. Any day now he would be feeling better; he would straighten up, he told her so.

Flying Low

Guy

🕯 He was frightened by his own furniture. He swore 🕯
it moved of its own accord. For years now, he wanted a
new bureau because of shadows the old one made on
summer evenings. He knew what lay low to the floor, what
slid along the woodwork. And this was daily life, a skir-
mish in the corner, a triptych of something plain, how a
single fry pan would be three, how a bureau would multi-
ply and tiptoe across the room. The house gave him no
rest but its heat or its coolness, its colors—maroon green
gray and his wife's crazy idea of some bit of pink—made
him reel in its stuffed presence.

He came alive in the streets. That's where his life
was (he saw it out there, Guy Hallissey's life, it was
strolling along the sidewalks and singing out loud), as if
someone left it there, and he had to go back out to get it,
flying low in his car.

Just gliding into Joe's Texaco where they took good care of him and every last cylinder of his crest blue DeSoto, or walking past Nicky's Shoe Service where they knew every color of his shoes, or sitting in the Palisades Cafe talking to anyone who came along across the Bloomfield Bridge to Liberty Avenue, where everybody knew his name backward and forward, made him feel like he was whirling, go-lucky, the wind itself. It was June of 1952. And if he wasn't there, it wasn't a party. Everybody said so.

He came home late for supper, or way past redemption in the middle of the night, smelling of some dim-lit place. He came home too loud, ringing the doorbell at 4 A.M., hoping to wake her so he would be less scared of hallway shadows, the smell of his own skin as if someone else were there beside him.

But then it passed. All he had to do was outlive a few moments, battle some little monster whose life span was a matter of seconds, and then he'd be fine. Everything would fall back into place. The scent of the house would rise up around him, fit him like a good suit (smell of her soap, candied scent of his children), making it not so bad, making it all laughable, why was he so scared.

She used to wait up for him, half asleep on the downstairs sofa. She used to have a thing or two to say, she would take him by the elbow into the kitchen, but not anymore. Except he could still hear her, telling him a thing or two in that sharp whisper, like a needle in the wind, she was poking at him, she was pointing out a few things he really ought to know.

He stood in front of the bathroom mirror and

43

listened. He was feeling cast out, relegated to his sins. He was the sum total of his sins, and he whirled right into them, with no choice but to choose himself, his own sweet skin.

He was a sneak and a liar, he knew it, and he was born, elated by his lies. No one came near him now. There was no way she could touch him. His whole body radiated heat. The bed was still with him. He was still in its warmth. It was hot and dry under his collar and he was breathing in his own sour heat.

He looked in the mirror and felt relief. He was far off, saved, from her awful adoration. He had no wife, he had seen to that, and certainly he was never meant to be a father, why he was just a boy himself. He would never let them get away with it, he would never let those three replace him in his own needed hierarchy. If it was up to him, he wouldn't give them another penny for all their rigmarole of bottles and clothes and little red wagons.

First comes me, he always told her that. It was just a little joke. But he was desperate for it now. For his wife's reprimands, for his mother's warnings he never even hoped to heed. He never even hoped to be good. He had given that up, and he longed for the door first thing upon waking.

He was awake now, and pure daylight was rushing into his veins like it was all new to him. He was doing all right; he knew what day it was and he was determined to stay put. But in his mind he could still see the wash rags, frayed, soaked with beer and dark with water, slapping the top of the bar where he had sat. That was all he remembered, the wash rags. That, and his hands holding

44

to the thick of the bar, the round sure edge of it, all nicked up and soft with age and the damp.

Who had he been with? Probably Willy Doyle, dear ole sonofabitch, who worked his life away at Joe's Texaco, a regular grease monkey on Baum Boulevard, but he was still worth a lot, and God knows how, but he kept his fingernails clean. It was Doyle for sure, and he saw him now in the one lone light of the Palisades Cafe. He liked seeing his big fat chin. He loved his friends; he touched their sleeves. I love you guys, he told them, This is the only place in the whole country where I could say that and I wouldn't be queer. Doyle nodded with his chin. The guy even waved hi with it, it was all lit up with stubble in the one lone light of the Palisades Cafe, or in a blast of daylight or neon from the opened door in the wind along Liberty Avenue.

Funny but he hated that, both daylight and wind rushing into a place from an opened door. How out of place the sunlight was, and night wind was cold under his collar, along the spine of his back. He hated being cooped up, except at the Palisades Cafe. He liked Saturday afternoons there, then pouring out the door in the middle of the night like the day never happened. Within the mustard-colored walls of the cafe in Bloomfield, just catty-corner to the house he grew up in, he was secreted away with no children or wife. There was nowhere to be but a bar stool. He was a good citizen of the Palisades and that was that. There was no world.

Daylight was like a blast of his wife's radio news in the middle of a good song. First thing in the morning like that. What a lot of jaw and no do from Joe McCarthy, all

45

the senators, and their micey lovers. Their brains were in their toes. Somebody better straighten things out and somebody better suffer (he smelled a rat in the butter), but he didn't give a damn to know who got slapped on the ass and elected or who got sent down the chute. He wished she'd turn the damned thing off.

At first waking the thought of a drink made him sick. It was a nausea that went skyward and umbrellaed over him. But at the same time that it made him sick, it made him eager, anticipating it, the moment, soon from now, when he would want it, another drink.

He stood in front of the bathroom mirror. His cuff was frayed, he saw that when he went to touch his head, to run his fingers through his curly hair. But then he stopped. He had slept in his shirt, it was more than wrinkled, it was trash, he thought. And his hair was getting thin. It was like a little joke the world was playing on him, and he felt a sudden resolve to visit his mother, in whose presence he could be as grand as a general, taking her by the elbow, guiding her across the street like she was his little girl.

Her hose would be rolled over laced shoes, he could see it bunched around thick ankles, and he knew who he was, a son. He looked in the mirror and felt dazzled by his own capacity to know this, for a single moment, that's what he was, a son. She loved him like the dickens. He always knew that. He grinned at himself. Loves me, he thought. Loves me like I discovered the egg, one lucky shot and there it was, pure perfection. He was capable of great things. He knew that.

But he saw her now, the early snow of her hair, her

46

face unbelievably round and pink like a baby doll's face. She was wearing black, though it wasn't supposed to go that way. She was wearing black and there was nothing he could do about it. Like all his life she was mourning some unmentioned that crept on cat paws out of sight but within the chambers of hearing. He knew it all along. Even as a dumb kid. There was something there. He was listening for it now.

He saw her. A good-looking woman, grim from years of auto parts. A large woman with thick soft arms, she lugged pails on Sundays and he hated that. He wanted to knock them out of her hands, swipe them off, pitch them from the window. She spent most of her life on assembly lines, at sinks or stoves, with a regular waste of time for a husband, and he hated all that, too. He liked to tickle her, sneak up behind her, get her going when her mouth was a perfect dash, her lips so buttoned up you couldn't even know she had lips. Whenever he tickled her, she'd tuck her head into her shoulder like a little bird, and shoo him off with her backside, waving her thick arms backward, her hands fast and bewildered. When was he going to stop that, take down the garbage for a change, and once and for all, after all these years, when was she going to get it across to him, she hated to be tickled.

He felt it under his feet, the edge from which he had fallen. You're nobody, he warned himself, and then thought better of it. And slam, there he was, squaring his shoulders, he could feel it, as sure as if he brewed himself up, a concoction, he made it up as he went along, a real contraption, somebody. He could make it happen.

He turned from the mirror and peeked at his wife

47

through the crack in the bedroom door, where she fit almost perfectly in her thinness. She was combing her hair, no mirror, just looking into air, putting on her lipstick, arranging her dress, tucking herself in. He stared through a sliver of light where the view was small and terrible, and he saw them, all three, one tugging at the hem of her dress, another one on the floor sitting smack down on his good Italian shoes, and the last of them, that little scrap of a thing, calling to her from the crib.

What had she done? His life was overrun with them. How was he supposed to pay? That little golden thing of a girl was plenty enough. And then what happened? Two more, and all he could see was a frayed cuff with ten hands wriggling out of it. And where was she off to now, packing them into their clothes? He would follow her, ballooning out at them from revolving doors, from behind telephone poles and the hauls of trucks. There were certain things he wanted to forget (three whole kids and the radio news) but there were certain things he had to know.

He was solitary and at the center of something, he could feel it, he was inspired. A man who was married to himself as the bear is married to the woods. Not responsible (he was out of his head sometimes, he knew it), but unredeemed. He peered through the crack of the bedroom door. Hounded by his own dogs, he sent them off in her direction, then lowered his head and reared against the enemy that was not there.

The country and the man suffered a similar illness. The era seemed to have memorized him or he had memorized it like the instructions of a terrible chore that

48

needed to be done, the chore of his own dissolution. The pieces that the country was in fit him. Though the country would fare better, bury its fear (moving further into it) with bigger weapons, and leave him behind, a trail of smoke with no children or wife. The men of good health, whom he resembled at times in bravado, in whiskey or lies, the generals, husbands, or senators, the men without a clue, in bar rooms and planning rooms, would continue to be born and raised, slapped on the ass or elected. He was no worse and he was no better than most, he thought, he was doing all right.

He lived well-liked in the backstreet hub and fuss of the neighborhood. He loved a good joke or a good parade, everybody trooping around, wearing something gaudy, waving something real. He always had a speech, something always in his honor, or a story to tell. Everybody took such gritty pleasure in hearing his newest or taking on one of his bets. Everybody told him so, if he wasn't there, it wasn't a party. No sense going without you.

But there was something inside him. He felt it now and it was not unlike the feeling he remembered from Saturday afternoons as a boy, slipping into a darkened church.

Red-knuckled Catholic in the punishing days, he took to off-color jokes on Sundays and a flip of the cards behind his mother's house, where walls were Cleve'd or Joe'd with wild blue signatures. Me + Me, he wrote in some poor whale of a heart, a cheap comic book scribble of some profound monster, capable of everywhere, dazzling in its capacity to be afraid. Boy of boys, showman on the cliffs of grace. What a pleasure to risk your soul,

49

catch hell, and with one wrong move to rid yourself of this slow measured box-step of grace, God's monotony, and know you'll be gotten for this, your daddy's own boy.

But then the feeling started at the tips of his hands, from the top of his head, from his toes, and settled dead center in the confessional in the pit of his stomach. He was following instructions now. He was doing what he was told to do. He was owning up. He heard it now, what crept on cat paws, and knew it was true: Guy Hallissey, son, brother, husband, and father, a handsome talented man, was a big disappointment. There was an edge, a beautiful height, from which he had fallen.

That there was someone else there listening didn't matter. What he felt was beyond having company. He could hear himself talking because he was talking to himself. The sweet-smelling priest, too thin and pale and too dressed in black, didn't matter. The sweet smell was coming from the priest's hands, a blur of white through the crisscrossed metal grate. When the priest waved his hands in front of his face in the form of a cross, the sweetness set off into the closed air of the confessional. His forgiveness didn't matter either. Mercy was out of the question.

I'm so ashamed, he said when he saw it. It was this. It was darting in and out of the darkness in the confessional. The loose fish of his soul, fast and frail. It was the tiniest thing.

He'd get himself out of this, hurtle headlong into space from Saturday to Saturday, a pure invention. Women would love him. Bleached cuffs would graze at the June air. Expensive shoes would gleam over hot concrete. He would slip off from himself into thin air. A new car every year would get him there. Or a storm of booze would do it.

As a boy, his sins were small, and as a man so were his violences, destroying only a marriage, a way of life, part of a legacy.

His illness, that despot of the house, was like the crocodile shadow cast out on a wall by a man, a monster to the body that is not.

It was nothing, he knew it, it was just a little sadness (root and fire of everything), just a little fear (it glinted like iron ore bedrocked in the veins of the earth). He'd get over it, he said, hammering at the toes of the thing that would outlive him.

When he looked in the mirror again, he thought of his father, something he hadn't done for years. His father was a gambler, a good-for-nothing, swinging in and out the door on a wave of whiskey to steal the money, kept in case of disaster or celebration, from the coffee tin on a high shelf. It made him laugh. His father was a short man and the thought of him climbing on a kitchen chair to steal quarters like a little hooligan was more than he could keep a straight face about. He grinned into the mirror. You're too pretty and too skinny to ever come of use, his father said that to him often enough. Having too many losses to keep to himself, he bet his son would lose.

Whether his father was refusing to work or dying young amounted to the same thing. It was up to him, a young boy who worked part-time in a drugstore, delivering small packages, obsessed with the unaffordable and the some-day-soon that would never arrive in the domino days. He should be in charge, no matter what his mother said. (I'll take care of it, she said.) With a sense of collapse that came and went like the presence of his father, he kept fifty bucks under the doily on his bureau all his working life so far, just in case. He would assure himself with this, this bird in the hand, something unstolen. At the last possible minute of famine or war, some of Moscow's monkey business or his own, he would be capable, having this, at least. Fifty bucks was a beautiful thing. Gorgeous, he thought, like a worsted suit, devil's food cake, or his sister, Helen.

His dreamy-eyed sister adored his good looks which resembled her own. She would die at thirty in a slanted tam, still dreaming of movie queens. She took their poses in penny arcades. Somewhere in a shoebox, in the back of his closet, all his life he would keep a seven-inch stack of those photo strips, four shenanigans a piece, where she stares at her endless self over bare white shoulders, from under various brims of switched hats, in the evening shade of glasses she wore under warm moons. His youngest looked just like her; Helen couldn't keep her hands off the girl, always had to have her in her lap, and it gave him an eerie feeling about time, like living in a hall of mirrors.

She was a good girl, his sister Helen. Without even a stick for a child, which was just as well. One thing he knew about his sister, when she walked she swam, then landed like a jet. She settled cross-legged on the sofa, like a bag of bright ribbons under lamplight. She would prepare a little ritual of popcorn, photographs, lamplight, and Louise, his youngest on her lap, and across the years they giggled together in awe of her image. This is your Aunt Helen; don't forget me; you look just like me, she would tell her. Aren't we beautiful? You just make sure: marry someone who knows it, someone who kisses you like me.

It was a waste of her long dark hair and her gray-green eyes, but she had married too young a renegade priest who never ran far enough away from the idea of a God who was clean, untouched by the likes of her. All that man ever really wanted was to die in the arms of God. His heart was white, she explained, like a bone.

A big sham. That's what he thought of his sister's marriage. The guy had no taste for women, didn't have a clue how to love them. He looked in the mirror. His life felt all muddied up like a chin. He was muddied up with other people's stories. He had this sense of history; it was breathing down his back, muttering into his ears with its crazy chorus of aunts and uncles.

Never married, they clustered together. Uncle George, Aunt Sal, Uncle Joe, Aunt May. They adored him at the center of their lives in a tiny fifth-floor apartment over Herron Hill, where windows were nailed shut and the smells of last night's supper and morning's bacon grease circulated through the vents. They went on binges of silence, tea cups of whiskey or Ovaltine. Nearly every Saturday he would visit. He never knew what he was going to find at the top of the stairs. The cat in the garbage can, the telephone's dying ring under a jungle of news-paper and doilies.

Red-nosed or pure white, pudgy and round as all creation or thin like dashes of salt, with hardly a word or with incessant chatter, they went to their own extremes. They sniffled, they shook, they pinched his cheeks, pointed to his ribs and fed him supper, they stomped off or sewed.

Aunt May was the only one with her own room because she was the one who sewed. She glistened, her forehead, even her lips, like a little saint bent over her stack of linens and shirts. Aunt Sal painted his picture with the jack of hearts. Keep still, she'd say, You're worse than a pogo stick. Uncle Joe muttered into his cup of Ovaltine, complaining of his reformation. His fingers, like the walls of the room he shared with George, were orange from years of cigarettes. Otherwise he was smoke white, like his sisters, a tall thin man in charge of groceries, who took endless street cars to markets and bakeries. No one was allowed to offer him a shot of whiskey; otherwise his dogged sweetness in lugging shopping bags would vanish on a dime. And Uncle George, well they let him be. He could drink whatever he wanted. No one could say anything to him since he was the one making money.

What a bunch of redheads, he thought, like they were all lit up from the inside, from the dry brush of their bones, and it bothered him, the thought of their thin bright hair. But he comforted himself, Why even our Lord Jesus was a redhead.

He looked in the mirror. Any minute now he would be feeling better, he promised himself that; he would go to the kitchen, he would have a drink, just a little in his coffee cup. And whatever happened, whatever he did, at least he had this: this woman wearing black, this slip of a

sister who thought she was French, this chorus of aunts
and uncles, this wife, that little golden thing of a girl,
were all crazy about him.

But he was flying off, fast and frail, he was burning up the
road. The road was like a ribbon in his head, unfurled,
blown this way and that, and he hugged to it.

The DeSoto hummed in the palms of his hands.
Heat rose up from the floor of the car and he could feel it
through his shoes. His white cuffs were rolled and summer blew like warm water into his sleeves.

June heat was like a body adrift on the outskirts of
the city, steaming up from the middle of the road, and the
grill of the DeSoto nosed straight through it, breaking
heat into little hot pieces. All that he passed and all that
he approached blurred with speed: trees, cafes, the colors of clothes. Black lightning of his wheels, and everything he lived was left behind, silent, not a peep, not a
color, just the road.

He would have liked to live like that, sharp and
clean and flying low. He would have liked to live like a
single blade of grass by the side of a blacktop road, a road
too overgrown now with flora and family stories, where all
these faces and voices rise up like summer heat, burning
into consequence.

Staying On

Anna

🜂 She wiped at the window beside the sink with the 🜂 hem of her dress, while the water rolled in its pot. The sound of boiling water, insistent, far off, seemed unfamiliar and she could not remember what it was she was supposed to do next.

From the window she spotted a cardinal, of all things, in what little was left of the snow, and held still, devoted to it, and then to the places where it had been: the empty bush, the black wire bobbing. Lately she stood by windows long after cardinals, alley cats, or clouds had come and gone, as she traveled back, slow but sure-footed, from the space between herself and nothing there, that stretch of silence, magnetic. Talking through the window into the cold yard scratched with patches of snow and yellow grass, Poor trees and bushes, she said to herself as if they were a race of people.

The water rumbled, inconsolable, in its pot. For the life of her she couldn't remember where she kept the sugar. So this was life, she thought, even supper had taken a wrong turn into the darkness around the corner where she could not explain.

These years of staying on were like a photograph of something that was just plain ordinary, but burning at the edges, she thought, as she liked to picture things in her mind: a bird, a bush, a bed with four legs, what she had made of the supper table, hurried with platters of beef and potatoes. (Food was the last thing she was able to give, it held them together, he needed to be fed.)

Or these years became a picture of him in her mind, where he sat on the beach, too thin and pale in cloudy weather, stranded there at the water's edge on the browning shores of Lake Erie in his bright red swimming trunks, black shoes and socks, with those awful red patches on the white skin of his legs. The state would not allow him in the waters of Erie anymore. Elbows on his knees, bony and off in the distance, he looked like some rare species of bird, so starved for the sky, he could vanish any minute into air, into something you could not call flight, only disappearance, a trail of smoke, with no children or wife.

He had a passion for water. For a moment in her mind she stood knee deep in Lake Erie, looking back at him sitting at the water's edge, and she wished it had been her, the one who was banned from the waters of

Erie. She hated water anyway. Sun, too, preferring evening, when he left.

Primping in the mirror like that at 6 o'clock, putting on
the dog, God knows when he'd get back, ringing the
doorbell at odd hours, rousting the kids. He had his key
but preferred to wake her. Singing out of tune, he came
home too loud, muttering and bumping, complaining
about the furniture, swearing that it had moved of its own
accord, or she had rearranged it behind his back, just to
make him a stranger in his own house. Off on a binge
again, with this end-all-and-be-all attitude about himself, he was preaching what she should and shouldn't do.

First comes me and then comes me again. He said
that from the first. (Only two weeks after they were married, and she was flabbergasted, but she always found a
good excuse. It was nothing, a morsel, a moment, poor
day, forgiven.) But she remembered it now like a clue, an
agate, some pure mineral that shone an answer.

She could no longer distinguish between the
crouched positions of the enemy and the beggar. Was he
dangerous or was he in pain?

He no longer wept at the edge of the bed. He was
fine, the doctors told her so. Only cruel now, he seemed to
be better, suddenly familiar in his drinking bouts and
infidelities. The wives of Franklin Way spoke at the edges
of their houses, on sidewalks, in the yards near winter,
breathing into their hands, stamping their feet; or in
summer, ruffling their dresses, rippling their skirts for
some blessed wind. They raised their voices in the middle of night, they slept on sofas, and in the morning they

cooked, they clanged the pots, they banged the lids. She stood at the fringes of their stories. It seemed at times as if they had all married the same man.

Years ago she took to sleeping on the downstairs sofa, to wait up for him, to make sure he was safe, and now it was out of habit, because the curves of the sofa had become more familiar to her than her own bed. She slept on the sofa, with the oldest, now seven years old, who insisted on it, climbing down the stairs in the middle of the night, curling up with her, into the valleys of her body. She thought of herself that way, as a valley, a hollowed-out space. She would wait up or not now, but she wouldn't say a single word.

She got out now whenever she could, in the afternoons, especially on Saturday. She hauled her kids down the twenty-four steps of Franklin Way and left their father sitting in his chair. As a special treat she took her three to the Penn Avenue underpass, where the trains came through overhead, on the way to her cousin's house with a week's laundry in her son's red wagon. (Her cousin had the only spin-dryer washer for miles around. It was a blessing in the family.)

With the two youngest heaped in the wagon with the laundry, they would stop and wait, overheated on the black tar, her hands changing from one head to another, her fingers always ticking at tables or on the tops of their heads. Helen stood on her own two feet, an arm's length from Anna, who taught her how to wait, to listen with her hands against the steel posts until coal, cattle, men careened into town and the overhead train shook down wind and sound and grit into the hot shade of the underpass. Eddy stayed put, just barely, with the youngest in the wagon. The girl was no more than a bump fattened with blankets and sheets and her father's green clothes, and the boy no less than a wild bundle of yelps and wriggles with short plump legs wrapped around his sister's sleepy shape.

When the train finally came, Anna tilted back her head, upraised, as if the sky were a book where she found what to say: Sounds like the Alleluia chorus, she told her kids, who screamed and clapped, except the youngest who slept even as the hillsides seemed to shudder down. Wave, wave, she told her kids. Somebody has to wave, the men get lonely.

Alleluia chorus, she told them, Wave. And while the youngest slept, her boy and her girl tilted their heads toward the sound of her voice mixed with the overhead train. Squinting in the sun, in the gritty current of the uncovered coal cars, she shielded her eyes. To her way of thinking, these were the plain hard engines of God. Penn Central. Lacka-lacka-wanna. South Pacific. Chessie Line. She felt a windblown peace in the furious presence of trains, in the departures and arrivals of the black rumbling engines, in their roar, a correspondence of change, a body blown forward; and she held still.

Trains headed out this way and that all over the city, northeast or southwest along East Ohio Street, past Lefty's Barbershop, Jack's Bar, Steel City Vacuum, roaring past hillsides gnarled with branches and dotted with houses. The trains blew by, discarding houses to their hillsides, looping along the edges of the city on the river lines, crisscrossing through the center, barrelling past neighborhood ladies who stood at crossings, leaning into space, with coats unraveled, their scarves asunder. Coming in from the darkness, stamping their feet, great black engines would break through narrow tunnels into their lives like the single word that solved a riddle. Trains blew by past crowds of rooftops, past shook cellars and chimneys shouldered into hillsides, changing the pure solid rock of the neighborhoods into motion, changing the held-tight, held-down quiet of their lives into sound.

Her boy and her girl rose up and hollered, until even the youngest woke, and they danced with the vibration, it shook their teeth, they shimmied, they stamped their feet, and it was her own fault; she had bred it into them, a great respect for trains.

Then rushed by the thought of laundry or supper, by some emergency of flight like the train-track wind they felt in her bones, Fort Pitt, she said, that's it, let's go. And they tilted their heads toward her, toward things they could not yet see, their eyes and foreheads swept clean of their hair. The wind blew her skirt into their faces and hands, and they did what they were told, they didn't beg her to stay, as the 3 o'clock train vanished overhead.

It was over. There were no more trains. Pittsburgh held still again and the smallest of sounds rose up from its silence; cups clattered down from cupboards again; feet walked the floors; water churned through hoses; and Penn Avenue in Wilkinsburg turned to salt and rock again and stood its quiet ground. She pulled them along on their way to Kensington Court, her cousin's green

61

world, and then to the dusty steps of Franklin Way, where they would find their father on his way out the door.

Let him go out if he needs to, she thought, they were better off without. Nearly every evening, he stood there in front of the mirror in his two-toned shoes, pleated trousers, and starched white shirt. It was suppertime and a storm of pins and needles was brewing. He waited before slamming the door. I'm married to me, he told her, and the door slammed.

She wouldn't eat a solitary thing all evening, not a slice of orange, not one skinny wing of that chicken, but feel this cliffside inside herself, the blades of rock underfoot, the emptiness of not a single green thing that grew in open sunlit space, where wind once blew apples from the trees. She was hungry and wouldn't eat her dinner. The roasted chicken could sit leftover in its pan, the cake stay solitary on its plate.

From the window beside the sink, she saw it then and knew what she had become. A wire stretched tight, bouncing birds from their perches, scattering her children into their books. She was the whole world to her kids, she knew it, she was the wind that turned it, and the hand beneath it, just in case. She was hard at work, in motion; the wind was sharp and dry; her children safe, well fed. The motion (she was rushing now, she was falling into herself) started from her toes, it weighted her arms, knotted her stomach, then caught in her throat as if she were supposed to speak.

But who could speak? Who had time for talking? Who could dare say a single thing about it?

But who did he think he was? Who was he, she wanted to know a few years later, parading his women like that in front of her children, to accuse her of anything? Hush, she told him, she would not have her children involved in these shouting matches. She was packing them off to bed at odd hours, surreptitiously checking for fever, especially the oldest, the one who could actually see things. The others were famous for amusing themselves, but Helen was forever planting herself in front of her, trying to protect her in her own baby way, her arms wrapped backward around her mother's knees, chin up, staring her father down. It was the last straw, a nine-year-old defending the space between them.

It was the last straw. Past suppertime. In her own living room. The woman was blond and she stood there, holding his hand. He introduced her to the kids as his new wife. I'm getting married, he told her, and we're taking the kids. He stood there and laughed, stood right there on her own carpet.

She looked at the leftover cage of the roasted chicken sitting on its platter at the center of the table. It was February of 1955. Shreds of dark meat lay on the tablecloth along the rim of the platter. At the sight of the chicken, with its little brown heart, she took the four corners of the tablecloth, one by one, and folding each to the center, gathered it up in her arms (the bones, the plates, the unmatched glasses) and, kit and caboodle, she said to herself, threw the whole of it out back in a black barrel.

Who was he? she wanted to know. Was he dangerous or was he in pain? From where she stood in the vortex of the storm, after ten years she decided: she would get her kids and herself out of this. And in twenty years or so from the date of departure, for no magnificently apparent reason but for a certain calm she felt in the way her furniture stood in place, she would be happy.

Anna, 1956–1957

In the Quiet

Anna and the Children

⬦ The colors of their tiny coats glittered at first ⬦
sight, then dulled to plain cotton hauled with its creases
from drawers, flattened by suitcases, wrinkled by
buses—but Helen, Eddy, and Lulie Hallissey caught in
sunlight were glorious, she thought, and the new of pink
yellow red, so long as it lasted at the corner of her blue
eye. It was nothing really. It was summer glare. It was
only a moment that cast light on their faces.

Anna Hallissey was on her own for the very first
time in Erie, Pennsylvania, on a two-day trip to the lake;
it was for their sake. The colors of their coats, the pressed
blue sky of August, wide without a wrinkle over gray-
brown water, made her heart fall backward, like a rare
somersault, as she blinked in the corners of sunlight, in
love with what was here and capable of leaving.

Their shy pink feet stepped from sandy curbs. Hesitant, skipping, looking both ways, they were stumbling into her toes, she was hugging their wrists. Listen, she told them. That rush of water in the silence. It was only for an instant.

Far below her on either side, one held to her skirt, the other to her hand; the oldest she had by the wrist in front of her and then let go. The oldest snapped her hand away all the while they walked. But she had managed it. They were safely across the street. And in the stillness of the other side, she could guess what they would have for supper.

She could see them (laughing, with their hot dogs and bright yellow mustard) to the smallest detail, sitting in their circle of three around the oilcloth-covered table checked with blue and white squares darkened at the edges, while she hovered above them, wiping her hands on a towel, and it grieved her in a funny sort of way, how life went on, even on vacation in Erie, the four of them in a too-small room, eating supper.

But she would amuse them. She would make this a happy day. After supper she would set them on her ankle one by one, on a little white horsey for a ridee ridee to town. They were too old for it, she knew it. God knows, even the youngest had to get herself to and from kindergarten this last year. (I'm sorry, it's necessary, you're a big girl, she told her, skimming her hand, apologizing for it.) And Lulie Hallissey went off each morning, a windblown thing, down Dorothy Avenue, looking back all the way to the very last second of the corner, while from the porch she shooed her forward with her hand, urging it into her, the will to do it.

68

They were good children. They did what they were told to do, and she wanted something nice, something once in a blue moon, to give them. They lay curved on carpets for hours at a time in their deep habit of quiet. Their tongues found their way to the bottom of their lips. They made valentines from paper doilies, infinite numbers of them, and always for her, way past February. I love you Mummy, they always told her that. More than anythink in the hole wirld. They snipped at magazine pictures. They colored like mad. But today and tomorrow, she was determined to give them two full days of sunlight in open air.

They would surprise her. Struck by sunlight from their quiet, they would be lifted, cured, and giggling, they would dive upward, burst forward, be quick from their chairs, recovered, at the sight of water.

She would follow their lead. She would raise her chin, and by the compass of their willingness she would traipse, hating the sunlight and even the thought of water, but loving the colors that light and the lake made of their skin and thin straight hair. She would be careful to count the stop signs, study the bungalows along the way, an orange flower pot on a kitchen sill, for the way back. Otherwise, unused to travel, her sense of direction would vanish like a bubble. Then what would she do? The thought of her voice asking for help in this strange land made her determined to find her own way.

She stopped. (The oldest was doing it again, she was pulling away.) She stood by a row of one-story clapboard houses. Painted white, they all looked the same and it made her dizzy. (Quit that, you stay close to me, Helen,

69

she told her and slapped her hand.) She made them wait and hold to her skirt, then the boy ran ahead like crazy. Running ahead like crazy, saying Hey, Watch me, why don't you? Anna's eyes were blue, ice blue and searching into the distance. (Eddy, you come back here right this minute.) Then he popped up like toast right by her side.

Tiny bungalows, she thought, disappointed. Slightly ramshackle and all the same by the brown water. But Anna Hallissey had a better, bluer plan for water. She had cathedrals while the world had bungalows.

The houses were set close to the broad street, with small screened-in porches tucked back at the sides, their steps speckled brown with sand. Beyond the houses, in the smallness between them, the open space of the lake was new to her. It caught her eye, pulling her out, into itself, where she didn't want to go. She would catch her breath. She would sit on the beach and go over it in her head, clapboard by clapboard, bungalow by bungalow, flower pot by sill.

They had made it this far. She was managing and allowed herself to look at the sky again. She stood there, her feet planted firm like a tree, with her hand on her hip, with her chin upraised. And there it was, only for an instant, pure beauty.

These years it had rarely happened to her that the sky, a color, a tree she met in life was larger, brighter, better, more blue or bent into green than what she knew with shut eyes. As far back as she could remember, winding her way through the streets of Pittsburgh where there was always something to adore, she would laugh at the lazy sound of her own petticoat—she would; and she was thrilled: a certain afternoon sky, stray dog or sleeping cat, a new set of streets on the mill side of town, the colors of steel mills flaring up between rivers and railtrack in rain, and returning home, a strange plum color her furniture cast in shadow; and she was thrilled.

But now a sadness always set in. She was walking along the course of an afternoon or these years, still capable of surprise, of joy even, like a low green water ebbing within her, and after the beauty of a mongrel, the pout of its face, after the deep gray thrill of Sacred Heart Church in Shadyside with its ribs of stone, its reach, there was a sadness, it was heavy on her eyelids, and she was no longer changed by the sky or a plum shadow. Beauty couldn't do that anymore, and she knew it. Nothing changed you the way sorrow or catastrophe did. And nothing was better than what she found in the darkness of her own shut eyes in the few moments she stole from pure air.

She patted their little rear ends, Let's go, she said, This is our lucky day, and they trudged forward. After something glorious, it was the same world, she thought to herself, and she was the same woman, her husband the same man. (She had left him sitting in his chair over a year ago, and he was weeping, but it was still the same. He was still her husband.)

She half expected to see him, poking out from behind a telephone pole or diving upward, a terrible surprise, from the middle of Lake Erie. (He did it all the time. He followed her. He would find her, he would take her to court he said, he would bring the priests.) But she knew what she would say this time. *Somebody*, she would

71

tell him (he was swimming toward her now in the smallness between the houses), was going to get taken to court
if this doesn't stop right now. She would settle it once and
for all.

Race, she almost said to them, lifting her hand,
ready to shoo them down the block. But she would let
them amble. They liked to kick the stones, they liked to
swing their arms through air, they liked to skip then
dawdle. She let them.

She was always pulling them along the streets of
Pittsburgh, hurrying their feet on the way back home
from the supermarket. She would get them on their toes,
clatter her little teacup feet and tell them, Like this, Run
like the dickens. She would tell them a lie, say it was a
race. Let's race, she would tell them whenever she saw
the turquoise of his Chevy, the white shirt, the hunch of
his shoulders against the steering wheel as he waited
outside the Giant Eagle Supermarket on Highland Avenue, beating out a rhythm on the dashboard, singing (he
actually had the nerve to sing). She cut across Highland
on the diagonal in the middle of the block and all the
while down the long stretch of Elwood Street his car crept
behind them, with the radio turned low. On cat paws,
insistent, he would not let go; and she shooed them
forward, like butterflies, she thought, in their colored
jackets. With her arms wrapped tight around brown paper bags toppling with cans, her hands waved them on at
intersections, searching from under bags of groceries for
their heads bumped this way and that. Their hands fluttered like eyelids. She jingled her keys to make them

hurry. Get inside, she told them. When the fat brass lock tumbled into place on Dorothy Avenue, she breathed.

But they were slow as molasses now, and they poured themselves sweet down the bright streets of Erie. One time, she remembered it now, she pulled the drapes and herded them into bed in daylight. She picked them up (they were too old for it) and lay them down. I don't care what time it is; we're going to bed. But like a bat out of hell and with an Oh My God, we forgot our prayers (a prayer of thanks for another happy day, she had thought at the time and laughed, she really did laugh), she jumped from her bed, she gathered them up, she held their hands, In the Name of the Father, the Son, and listened while they prayed. With an eye on the door, Mea culpa, she thought, she would sit in empty churches, she would kiss Mary on her beige china lips, she would eat priest bread.

Sunday mass was a terrible thing. And as she walked along the streets of Erie the far-away smell of incense, the underwater smell of churches, made her head reel. He had moved to their part of Pittsburgh. He had joined their church. All of a sudden there he was one Sunday at the 10 o'clock. She caught the corner of his shiny blue suit behind the stone pillar speckled with silver. And Holy Mary, Mother of God, she had said at the time, he was coming around with the collection basket of all things, her children were dropping their little green envelopes of quarters into his basket, and all she could think of was his brand-new turquoise '56 Chevy, and child support payments, how he never managed to make

73

them. She lowered her head. She put her arms around her children's shoulders, she jumbled them up.

He was gone now. He was behind her now. It was August in the streets of Erie and she was on her own. As they crossed the street to the beach, she put her arms around her children's shoulders. She lowered her head to hug them, she jumbled them up inside her arms, snapping the white pearl from her ear, and her youngest (with an eye held close to her cheek) saw it, the lobe bright pink like a punishment.

The priests had come and gone. She stepped up onto the curb and blessed relief, she said to herself, because she was rid of the earrings and didn't know what she was thinking of, wearing them to the beach in the first place. Priests, she said, hopefully she had put an end to that, too.

He had brought them to the house on Dorothy Avenue twice already. Married forever in the eye of God, they wanted her to know that, and she knew it was true. You're living in a state of sin, Father Rawley was certain of it. I have no thoughts of ever marrying again, she told him. Mrs., said Father Rawley. He would consider excommunication if she didn't go back. Your place is with him, he told her, He's a good man.

She remembered she breathed then a single breath. She took it from the air around her, it was blowing in from the yard where her children played, where she had sent them (Get outside, your daddy and his priests need to see me again), where they sat cross-legged in a circle, tribal and decided with fistfuls of earth, where they made priests into grass and brushed them from their clothes, where they loved her more than God. She took one good breath. I'm sorry, Father, but you're not a mother. She asked them to leave. She bowed her head and thanked them. Thank you, Fathers, but you're not mothers.

At the side of her eye she could see him slouched on her green sofa, with his legs flung open, pretending he belonged there. Look, she told him, These are the rules when you want to see the kids. He was reading the bottom of her knickknacks. He was spitting into his handkerchief. My husband, she thought. Even if she never saw him again (which she preferred), even if he never again roared up to the curb to visit her children. But they were his children, too. And she told them so. He's still your father, no matter what he does or doesn't do.

Either the world was ultimately small and disappointing, she decided, or her dreams were impossibly large and out of place. (She dreamed a cathedral, she dreamed a woods, blue lake; he would never find her there.) Either her dreams were just plain silly or learned of God and the stuff of angels. What could be better in a time of need than this cathedral looming at the tip of her nose, this deep woods nestled in the palm of her hand? Nothing, she thought. Except for love, she said, of her three.

This was more than she could imagine. At times she did not feel capable of its immensity but preferred to settle on a stitch, a sandwich, a blanket, a sweater, a plum. Their small needs saved her from that precipice where she loved them, or where she loved her father, or her husband once, above all things. Her husband needed a strong cup of coffee with five sugars. Her father needed a weak cup of tea, mixed with four sugars and Carnation evaporated milk. She would pour the tea for her father, she would pour the coffee, she would save herself.

Even as a girl (before they met, before she fell in love) she understood, from her third-floor window over Manon's Drugstore, how space extended, how worlds unraveled into worlds, and in the middle of it all, there was something glorious: the comfort of her own face. She saw it swimming there in black window glass. The sky was just too large, and love, she thought, it was all a whirl; it caught her eye, it tugged at her sleeves, pulling her out, into itself, where she didn't want to go. But she did, she went. And, she could feel herself walking, floating really, above her smallness in a cotton dress, alone on a road too wide and long and too silent to mention more than once or twice in this life.

But with three kids now and on her own, there just wasn't time for the sky, and it suited her fine, it saved her. She took in ironing, she washed her neighbor's floors. But she did promise herself a few things. One, she would make a cake for her kids every two weeks, it was important. Two, she would raise them to be good people. Three, she would make herself go bowling every Tuesday night, she would buy new shoes and force herself. And four, she would get them across the street.

They were not quite there but the sound of water was larger now and they did, they quickened their step. Growing lighter from their toes upward, they would, they would be happy. But then she thought of supper again and she knew it was true, her oldest did not like hot dogs. She could see it now, she would have to walk from place to place, reading menus out loud until they agreed. Helen should have whatever she liked. And in the long search for supper, for something that would please all three, the familiars of home had come to Erie, to this strange land. Even on this vacation, the first and probably the last, there was the nagging plainness of home, in the calls to supper, in the lugging of things, in cans of soup and changes of clothes, in thoughts of great sorrow or marriage. And there, on their way to the beach, at the top of the road, a church wedding of all things, in Erie. People actually married in Erie. They didn't come here just to die in the sun but to marry.

She felt a sadness for the women young and old in their once-a-year hats, for the grandmothers in their girdles, the men stuffed in their navy blue suits in August, the children stiff and poking from their clothes, for the hot imagined room cramfull of someone's distant cousins coming out of the woodwork, lingering at the heavy buffet, and she felt a sorrow because of the spoons, too small and squat, lost in their dishes. At the sight of a church wedding, she imagined the thin little man and the tidy laced bride, their life filled with Sunday visits to a sister's place, filled with birthdays and funerals and washed-down walls, their life in a quiet neighborhood of good people quick to casserole dishes; it insinuated itself, it rose up, and for a moment, her whole family, all her duntes, her cousins, her sister's kids, and all the neighbors with their eyes out for her children, had come to Erie for a polka wedding. She hated weddings.

This tired body was everywhere, she thought, lugging the suitcase filled with God knows what, like coats in

August they didn't need. But she wasn't going to let that bother her. In the back of her mind was the plain singular comfort of one's own bed in a rut far away, the dust and travail of home, the oiled rim of her father's brown hat where he tossed it always upside down on the kitchen table, her children's white spreads, their overstuffed beds, or her own thin narrow one, pulled from an upholstered chair. Her bed was a little out of place, neither here nor there, jutting out on the catty-corner in her daughters' room, but the sun came to wake her there and it was hers, one glorious thing.

They made it to the beach. A single cloud rolled overhead, then another. She stepped onto dry sand, her feet sank down, her shoes filled with it. But why did she know these things, she wondered: the miracle of bed, a shaft of sunlight at its foot, how beautiful a hat could be? Where did they come from, this woods or cathedral, this shaft of sunlight from infinite space? Someone had given them to her, she was sure of it.

She stepped across the beach, and decided: she was the one who knew. And she was the servant of her own creations, she owed them something, a story, a word here and there, and no matter what to never lose it, this joy of closing her eyes, of taking the day, the endless flat of the lake, a teacup, a frayed cuff, into the quiet.

They made it to the lake and she could feel the wind too cool on the backs of her children. They spread pink towels midway between the water and the streets of Erie. She sat on her ankles. She looked at the sky. She gave each cloud the evil eye, banishing each one to a small high place. She was determined to give her children two full days of sunlight. Kneeling on the beach she would take her time with the sky. She would listen for any hint of rain, her ear pressed against the hard side of heaven. (And there was a hard side, she had always known that, she just preferred not to admit it.) She would will the sky to be gorgeous, a hot bright weather for her three. Rain would throw them to the wolves, to their small room, and she would not let it happen.

One cloud, like one sadness, was a domino, toppling down all the others. But she would be a landscape with lake, a narrow strip of land, ax-shaped and sunlit, where they would live protected against truiuul strangers bearing bad news, where she too would live protected, in the pure culture, the shelter, of herself.

With a sense of beauty that was almost tyranny, Here comes Mr. Sunshine, she said. She insisted on it. And they knew it wasn't true. They could feel it in their sleeves, close to their skin, a chilled sky, the wind tipping up the hairs on their arms. But she was born to testify to the travels of light, the way it rises, abides on windowsills, the way it falls into a room, that flourish there far away on her nice clean woodwork, she could see it in her mind, that shadow of the window cast on her bed, and she was happy.

She was happy because of the way light fell on some poor thing, on some fortunate spot in their new place, apartment number 1 on Dorothy Avenue, or simply for the lack of something terrible like a cracked basin. They had four whole rooms, a whitewashed cellar, and a big green yard. The house gave her confidence with its wide front porch, its three gray pillars. She sat there on the beach and remembered it. She placed it right there at the water's edge in her mind and remembered the first time she saw it.

They drove from one neighborhood to another, from Wilkinsburg to Shadyside in her brother-in-law's Oldsmobile, from a narrow red alley to a tree-lined avenue. He was in real estate and he had found it for them. Good rent was all he told her, two bedrooms, and a big yard for the kids. Her children were all pinched down in the backseat, with bent elbows and crumpled knees, with ankles fallen into shopping bags, packed in with every last inch of what belonged to her now, with everything she took: their clothes, her duntes' blue vases, her books, a little red wagon, and them. They were all pinched down. She could feel them there in between her fingers, little warm pinches of dry brown sand, little salty buds, her babies. But at first sight of 713 Dorothy Avenue, its steep slope of front yard grass, its set of steps with curves of cement on either side, she could feel a commotion behind her head, and they rose up, they fell open, born, hers. Green and hillbound, they swooped down the grass. $100 a month, her brother-in-law told her and she nearly hit the roof. It was just too beautiful for them, she thought for an instant, how could they pay? But it was theirs, she knew it. They must be beautiful, too. She would manage it, and her dad would help; he'd come along.

The gray house on Dorothy Avenue between Elwood Street and Rosary Way towered over front yard grass. It was huge, it was grand, and it sprang for them from the side of her head, where their eyes had settled on her wavy hair, where the grass edged in, bursting into its hill by her right ear. They were all squinched down; they sprang forward. And what they felt, they knew it was a kind of grace, their very first touch of it. It was a wild feathery thing from their feet upward, from the sky downward, and they were chosen by this flourish in the air, this commotion at the side of her head, that made this hill, this house appear.

Their lives would begin where this house stood. She decided right then and there. For every week that passed, she would let them know, All my children are special. We are all special people around here. We're doing fine.

And so she was determined for their sake, nearly every day of her life, to fall in love with something plain that was set upon a table (a bowl of yellow flowers, a sack of sugar, a stack of white linens). And though it was a sorry thing (plastic flowers, a sad sack, a stack of used linens), her mind embraced it, whatever it was, it was hers, she had bought it with her own money, she had touched it, cleaned it, put it where it belonged, and she would not cast it away. Not a single thing would be lost to her, but it would shine, peculiar, hers, one of a kind, it would live up to her expectations, and she would be happy.

But they knew it wasn't true. (The flowers were faded, the linens worn thin, the sugar damp and clodded. And they were a bother, they could feel the downturn of their lips, pouty and particular. They were hungry, they were cold, they were hot and insistent. They tore their clothes, they refused to wash their hair, and she was bereft of something, out there in the distance, that they could not see.) They knew it from somewhere, in the way her eyelids fluttered down and shut, in the quick butterfly of her hands over their backs, in her tiny breaths hurried like the cat's heartbeat, from her very own bones, the back that stiffened at the sink.

Sometimes she stood at the sink and watched them playing in the yard. She sat on the beach; she stood at the sink. She watched them at their constant play: in motion, forgetful and stained with grass, or mute and concentrated on baseball, with brown tousled hair, bent shoes, naked knees, their shirts coming loose at the waist. And she saw, as in the momentary passing of a cloud, who they were for an instant only in her mind, where they stood quite still in a row, all bundled up in dark winter coats, with a trace of snow on their shoulders. She saw them through some accident of light that made them appear (they had his face) as the makers of her sorrow, the bearers of it, with nothing ahead of them, nothing else they could be. She caught sight of them in some far-off place, their eyelids shut against the wind, their hands and cheeks exposed. And there it was, her loss, it was speckling their shoulders, shutting their eyes.

At times when she watched them play, their joy seemed like such a noisy rambling out-of-order thing, a dangerous intrigue, and she wanted to make them hush. Don't you come in the house with that. Don't you Hi Mum me. Don't you step on my portulaca. You know you just can't go around breaking glass. What made you go and try a stunt like that? You'll rile up the Natalis' dog. Not in the house, you don't. And don't you start with me.

As she watched them play, she remembered herself in a red dress at twenty-one. Fire-engine red. Busty and

82

beautiful, he said too out loud and wagging his head, and the visiting duntes were shocked. She was slipping out the back door over Manon's Drugstore, slipping past her chores, and she didn't care a fig; she was racing down the stairwell, flying out the door. He was behind the wheel, the bend of him, his length, his foot on the gas. Joy was a dangerous thing. It made her slip out the door again and by the time she came back in, she had three children and she was alone.

She sat on the beach, clutching her purse, tucking her skirt down over her knees. She was sitting right beside them but they could see her far off from them and on her own. They were not enough to keep her here, they knew it. But then it did, the sun came out, just as she said it would. And they saw it was true. The clean linens stacked tight, bright sugar, the odd china pieces, cracked, but seamed with glue. Her idea of flowers on the painted sills. The squeaking of laundry lines on a good hanging day. And they were happy. They were all special people. They sat on the beach and looked at the sky. A good hanging day, she told them. Nice blue lake, she said.

Rinso white. Rinso blue.

They could hear her now. Every Tuesday after school.

Happy little wash day song.

And they smiled. It was what she wanted. The mint-pink towels, her new yellow stove, her duntes' vases crackled

83

with age and vague with painted flowers swimming over the watery blue surface, slid into view. Pastels (she had conjured them) swam through air to the hazel, blue, green of their eyes. And they smiled; they meant it.

The sunlight shifted to the water's edge. She sat on the beach and smiled, promising herself just one thing. She would sweep them off their feet and carry them, all three, her bundle, her bunch, her sweet potatoes she said, from one spot to another, right there by the water's edge, into the sunlight. She would follow through with it. From sugar to sunlight, from blue vase to the lake (although it wasn't blue, they knew it wasn't), from linen to moonlight. She would see to it, she would get them there, and they would be happy.

She was off somewhere again. They could feel her leaving, with that tilt of her head, with that smile on her face. But the stacked linens, the eye of round, the frosted cake, the lessons in stirring, the kissing of salty skin: this was solid evidence. She had been there once and they sat among the evidence of her days.

Let's go, she said, and they were stepping through sand. She was walking with them to the water's edge. They were here and they were there at home, stepping among her things, hushing through the kingdom of her house. They were in a place of beauty. They had followed her there, their hands groping along some invisible thread she had spun. They were studious, careful, groping along behind her, among the vases, linens, the cakes. They were sifting through sand at the water's edge.

They knew enough. They were cautious. It was many colored. It was hot and cold through their fingers.

They were working on it. They were sifting through. She was sad again. She looked at the sky. I take an immense amount of pleasure in my three kids, she said (she almost whispered it, to the wind as much as to them) and hugged her knees. They were sifting through sand, the bright and dark specks. They were digging now, and the bones of their fingers were chilled, digging the warm speckled things.

They would keep it in their minds, the vast stretch of brown sand, the day threatening light then dark. They would keep it for another time, for another place past childhood. Someday they would look back and find themselves ready in buckled shoes, ankle-deep in the shadows of front-yard bushes, afraid at the thought of buses, of full sunlight where they didn't want to go, but eager for it too, for the roar of buses over new highways, to be herded in, stepping high, settling in with the smell of baloney sandwiches; and they would find themselves in sunlight, cross-legged on the beach, with the bones of their ankles chilled, burrowed down into wet sand, with a man's black radio burning Buddy Holly into their ears (they laughed, they did); and they would know what they sprang from, where their roots were, spread wide and vast and unresolved, there in the quiet, swirled round with rock 'n' roll, there in the cold, in the hot speckled things.

She sat with them in the sand by the in-and-out water, in the here-and-gone sunlight. Her skin was white and trailed with a delicate leafwork of blue. They worried over her skin. She worried over theirs. She buttoned their shirts. They went to fetch her sweater from the bag and passed the man with the black radio. He was wearing his socks, singing into the air, and they laughed, they jiggled, they danced. They looked to find her again.

She was sitting there alone at the water's edge. They were walking toward her, dragging their feet, trailing her sweater through the wet sand, and the white sleeve dampened and smudged. They hesitated, they ran, they stopped to watch. They let her appear, come into being as they watched. She sat on her ankles. She breathed and rose higher. She was forming herself slowly, bone upon bone, by the water with her too-white skin. With one good breath, then another, she was growing larger and they watched. And someday, they thought, because of water, because of Buddy Holly and Dorothy Avenue, because of miracles and good intentions, because they understood change, because she breathed, she would be lifted, cured, and diving upward, she would laugh, recovered at the sight of something they could not yet see but knew in their own bones as a moment, a flourish in air.

They sat down next to her. And Helen, Eddy, and Lulie Hallissey's definition of heaven fixed itself there in their minds. Heaven was little; it was tribal; it was Anna at the center of their circle of three. It was the days and days with her.

How out of place she seemed in sunlight, braving it for their purposes, clutching her purse. (When it came right down to it, they preferred their room. They liked motels. They liked to belly down on floors, whisper nonsense and kisses into the palms of her hands.)

But they patted the earth for her sake into gateways, into towers. And she was half-hearted. She patted the earth into turrets and smoothed the walls. And no matter what was true, they would make castles. She would poke in the windows. They would trail their fingers along the flat for narrow winding paths. Because she knew that's what they wanted. Because they knew that's what she wanted. A Lake Erie castle: by the dark brown water, she said to herself. By a blue water's edge, they thought later, all tucked into one bed. They would be warm as pennies and imagine it there.

Even in their small room, if it came to that, she would amuse them, she would tell them stories. Listen how the children gallop in their shells, in their pudding bowls and from them, into the streets, into their lives, with the lessons of the woman they lived with. She would take the smallest thing and turn it into a kingdom. She would tell the truth, hold the shell, the cup, the furnished soup ladle to their ears. And in the quiet she would tell them, Listen for the wind. Listen how the ocean lives in our belongings. This storm is in our cups.

Listen, she would tell them, and they would learn. Of the days and days, of surprise departures and arrivals long in coming, of speed, the travel in all things, skyward perhaps or downward, something beyond the touch of their own small fingertips.

She would catch their eye, tug at their sleeves, she would pull them out, into herself, where they wanted to go, where she didn't want to take them, into that dimlit place, into the past. But she would, she would let them, if only for a moment, she would let them come to her, she would take them in. Listen, she would tell them and let them go.

What She Knew

Anna with Louise

⌷ At the touch of wind from an opened window, at ⌷ the smell of onions welling up from her good iron fry pan in summer, for no reason really, when the yards grew silent and the kitchen held still, she knew where she stood, on what ancestral ground of duntes and their sacred admonitions. It didn't happen very often or last very long, but there was a moment, and it was odd, appearing as it escaped, unlivable beyond a second in June, when they stood immense atop a hill with knotted hair and dresses blowing, and she knew.

Her youngest, her seven-year-old (her five-pound bag of sugar) who always stayed close in the kitchen on Sundays, lay humming under the table, with her nose stuck in the pages of the Sears, Roebuck catalog. Her girl was free to do as she pleased but she never seemed to want to do a single blessed thing on her own, stray too far off into sunlight, into the yard, or across the street into her own choices. When Anna saw her there, Rambler After, she sang through the window above the sink, Rambler Ever After Me, my little Lulie. And the girl laughed. That made it real. The sound of her girl laughing made standing at the sink real.

But then the smell of onions again (the yards grew silent, the kitchen held still) and her glances flew like ribbons through the window space, into the side yard, flying past Mrs. Natali at her sink next door, beyond the grass and brick, and wandered, far out into the clouds, to the sky and something small within it, a dot, reflecting from her own blue eyeglasses.

She had been raised in the silence of her father, and she felt it all around her now like the wings of a fly, it was buzzing. She stood at the sink and listened to it, and then to the clanging of pots in the hands of his large sisters, the Duntes Fritz and Simmons. The duntes made their houses large with the smell of onions. Early evenings, their houses drifted out into Oakland, on the east side of Pittsburgh, into neighboring yards. The smell of onions frying in butter drifted up back steps into other kitchens, even the streets were filled with it, making home of sidewalks and under hedges on a summer's night.

In her life with the duntes, where she was shuttled from one to the other after her mother's death when she was three, supper was the largest sound, the pot, the dish, the spoon, and not the human voice, which if it spoke, spoke of some necessity to begin. Or to stop: especially

89

that giggling of hers in back bedrooms with cousins who bloomed in taffeta dresses.

She wore what they gave her to wear, and then she danced in it. On the dining room table, where the uncles would lift her to give them a show, some German song, when the strudel was good and the ale was enough to forget their day at the slaughterhouse.

From pig to bacon at Armour's packing plant on East Ohio Street was an amazing thing. Cows and calves marched straight off railway cars into the hide house. Clubbed, refrigerated, and packed, they told her. And she knew what lay beneath the days, behind each work or song, within the lifting of buckets, the washing of walls; even supper had its great sorrow when the uncles came home imitating the bloody sides of beef, dead pork pieces caught in their cuffs. In the trolley ride home from the slaughterhouse to a set table in a wallpapered room, she saw how far they had traveled, from their birth among the trees and their apprenticeships at tailor and bakery shops in a small German town, to a city of eternal smog snarled with headlights and dark at noon, to railtrack and flood-water, to houses, flimsy or brick solid, boxed on steep rises, with windows amazed by steel mills.

With laundry on the lines above their heads, with whiskey, fish, and concertina, her family came in steer-age to the blank slate of this country, and every day, she decided, should be like this: another miracle, the first sighting of land. Though she hardly remembered it, being three. It was something she made up later, deciding how it would be. With only salt sticks in her father's pockets, in 1925 they arrived, their trusts with the world rearranged shortly after with the furniture, when her mother died from the long effort of ships and birth of the last child. The three children were divided between the Duntes Fritz and Simmons; she was packed off alone to the house of Eva and Josef Fritz on Cato Street.

The duntes told her: Your mother was a good woman, a hard little worker; she had a plain face, kind heart, small lungs, and a hatred of water; you're just like her. She looked at the photograph in her mind. A hazy brown, a forehead, with thin hair yanked back tight, a tiny woman in plain dark clothing. Like a little wren, she said to herself, and kept her, unmentioned, a thin shadow like blown smoke that would be forever sweeping the yellow bricks of a walkway to a house no longer there on Ward Street in Oakland.

She stood at the sink, washing colored Melmac. She never minded that she didn't have a mother. You just didn't miss what you didn't have, she thought, stacking the Melmac without looking, knowing in her fingertips how it fit on the sinkboard or in the cupboards, and she concentrated on that, counting the plates.

She stood at the sink, counting dishes. Her girl had nearly vanished under the table, except for the humming she had become. The humming reminded Anna to look, and there she was, at the side of her eye, like the dot reflecting from her blue eyeglasses.

Five-pound bag of sugar, my little Lulie, she called out into the air, That's how big you were, that's how you came to me, just as little and just as sweet. And the girl laughed. What a nice little shape you have, she told her,

91

lost for a moment in the thought of her small body, traveling years to get back to her, as the girl traveled forward, growing into another time, dreaming only of the future from the pages of the catalog, of trousers with tiny pink mice stitched on the pockets.

The girl floated off with the sound of her humming. Anna stood at the sink and Dunte's porch in Oakland felt like sand under her feet again. And from the faucet, in the rush of hot water, she could hear the blast furnace of Jones & Laughlin roar.

The porch at 216 Cato Street in Oakland had been painted gray, she liked to imagine it, the color of space and its constant rains. It was Saturday in her mind, so Dunte Fritz hauled a bucket of water from the cellar sink, swooping sideways through narrow hallways, warning everyone, If you're out you're out, if you're in you're in, I'm washing the porch. On hands and knees, in the dark hilly wind she called it, Dunte Fritz scrubbed in great confident circles, interrupted by the sight of distant trolleys with their lights still lit at 11 A.M. in winter, or here and there by a human figure in its unearthly passing along smoky Cato Street, and she stopped to puzzle out the fuzzy contour of a head of hair from a patch of lawn, to worry out the legs from their blend with hedges, and called Hello; it was the world again, risen from the residue of Bessemer steel.

Porch boards appeared under warm brown water. It was Dunte's porch again, and she referred to it that way the rest of the day, Don't muddy my porch with your feet. And it *was* her porch, Anna thought, Dunte made it so, through years of weekly scrubbings. Each board, each nail must have been a picture inside of her, something she knew from memory.

Anna's own memory of the house on Cato Street unfolded as Dunte Fritz swept through it with a slosh of water in her bucket. She could feel the house illuminated by water, growing in the shade, under cover of Dunte's large hands, its colors told and the ways of its people revealed, how their feet traveled its floors, how their bodies burrowed into its couches. Knowing the house, its couches and woodwork, under her hands, Dunte knew its people, the sadness of their clothes flung empty over the arms of chairs, the blind rush of their fingertips flying across the walls, flicking on the lights. It was Saturday, Dunte Fritz hauled water, and she knew. She knew to measure and to sift, to judge and to clear, to sort, and in an instant she knew what to save and what to let go, aware of what was possible, aware of what was lost. She knew necessity, when to pick and to strip, what to toss back. She matched and she fastened and she knew.

It was Sunday night now in Anna's mind, so Dunte Simmons soaked the clothes all night and knew. She boiled them each Monday with dark brown chips of Fels Naptha soap. Fels Naptha was poison, she told the children. She chipped it carefully with a knife into the boiler. In a haze of hot water, with a long thick stick Dunte Simmons lifted steaming sheets and clothes from the copper boiler then set them through the wringer. The shirts she starched with Niagara from a green and white box in a white enameled pan with a red painted ring around the edge, and pulled them again through the wringer before stretching the line in the yard.

The duntes were large women. Big-boned, beef-trust ladies, they called themselves. They were always hungry. But it seemed to her it was not what they ate but what they knew that made them large. Everything in the house bore witness to just a moment ago. The slouched hollowed-out pillow to a moment of rest, of happiness even, but already a relic, it was a thing of the past, a little grief that told of departure, the mindlessness of the living. What was slouched would be puffed up, what was hot and dirty, cooled down and washed clean. The duntes sped through their housework, erasing time, the evidence of human frailty, the need for food and rest, erasing tracks that seemed to pass not just from one room to another but from one life.

They arranged and rearranged until they got to some bare notion; they placed the vase of flowers not here but there where the extravagance of orange lilies spoke the plain truth against the white hall.

The duntes swept their porches daily. Weekly they dampened torn pages of the Pittsburgh *Press* and wiped at flowered carpets, absorbing mill dust so thick that it would blacken the hem of your slip on a walk from Cato to Bouquet. Monthly they hauled their carpets to the yard and beat them with the sides of brooms. When Dunte Fritz bought a hand sweeper, their lives changed.

They had more than most. Yearly the duntes banded together to clean the good wallpaper, thank God it was washable, they had the best of things. Starting at the ceiling, they made a ten-inch path with the gray clay, rolling it down the walls, stepping lightly on their toes over the carpet, careful not to track the bits of clay that broke off when they tried to make it go too far, kneading it like bread, until it was impossible, until it was black, then taking another clean handful that smelled of camphor, starting at the ceiling, clearing another path, a pure ten inches.

She learned from the duntes, she knew it all still. There was speed and patience in her heart, and mildew any moment now in the laundry bag. Still to this day, she never let her dampened laundry sit, especially in summer. And still she knew the taste of sugar water and how the dipped handmade doilies dried and stiffened on the line. There was progress, and by the inches a path was given in the wilderness of houses where doilies lay flat. And in her mind again, she was counting, bing bing bing, the numbers along the frame of the curtain stretcher; first you do the top, slipping lace curtains over the nails, then you do a little bit each side, left right left right and finally the bottom. It was satisfying. It was clear. Their furniture would last forever and their lives would go on quietly in good order.

And she had helped, her heart was to the wheel, she loved to be good. The corners of sofas and floors taught compassion, held secrets; there was grace in the turns of the rocker; humility and pride in the scrub rags; direction in the rungs of chairs; there was contemplation of infinite space in the corners of the floor; a great silence in the whirl of the vacuum suddenly ending; and the house felt flung open to its sky. She stirred and chopped and wiped, learned what spoons and knives and rags were for, and weight, it was to be lifted. It was another clean day with the duntes, another casserole, another pot roast, and cakes by the week. And so she was out there in front of the house again, picking up blown papers from Cato Street, because the duntes always said: People lose interest in the street once it passes their house. There was a certain way to do things to make life good. You took care of everything, that's what you did. And if you made a mistake, if you burnt a cake, you learned, you changed, you bent to the ways of the oven.

In 1930 her father remarried with supper as his reason. The stepmother she remembers in a snarl of smoke from the Pittsburgh mills is catching pigeons again in her mind, strangling wings in the cornered eaves with bare hands. Her skirt an avalanche of muslin, she climbs down the attic stairs with the success of the dead thing. With three syllables that cause the neighbors to straighten in their beds, she clarifies the situation: *Pluck, clean, boil*; then sits with her refusals: an empty oven, an unswept floor. She sits and has a dream how she was not born for this, for pigeon dinners, for three children ready-made and bursting from their clothes. She sits as if the fruit to which she gave birth was the kitchen chair. She recommends the salt, the cutting of feet first.

First thing they poke at you, toes of the ugliest walking creature on earth. She stood at the sink and remembered it. The pigeon lay on the counter top, on a yellowed Pittsburgh *Sun-Telegraph*. With the far tip of the knife, she straightened its toes, organizing the bird around its death. She was doing it all over again in her mind, handing the knife to her sister, Rega, who chops off the toes with her eyes shut. The gnarled stems of toes lay on the counter again, wilted and bodiless. She plucks gray feathers from a poor and private angry white. She salts the floor while the skin of the bird, that weekly prize, goes blue in boiling water. The slamming of the kitchen door is her one remark.

Rega stays behind and gets it done, and hates it all her life, requesting later a small low company of violins for the stories of her childhood, for pigeon dinners, for their dad's drinking bouts when he came home late stumbling into the furniture, for weekly cab rides in the night to 216 Cato Street where the children were sent every time there was a fight.

She stood at the sink by the opened window, wondering as she did sometimes where Rega got her stories, stories that she felt vaguely unfamiliar with. You were fine, Rega, and I was fine; we had our Dad; she had her problems; the world was round.

Pigeon dinners, though. That, she remembered. And she was out the door again, snatching her father's black umbrella from the corner of the porch, stabbing the wind. A perfect scribble in the coal-blackened air, she arrives, a piece of the weather, at her father's tailor shop on Bouquet Street, the bottom of her bloomers stuffed with buckeyes and gray with soot.

His fingers travel expertly over blue gabardine in a ritual of thread slipping in and out; his hands, those survivors, bob like corks on water. He is the color of dolls, his toes turned inward like a child's. Telling him anything suddenly, a short story of dead wings, the hope of a nickel for

97

a tablet, she can't stop talking, he won't begin. His shadow floats on the wall. He has moved an inch and this must be conversation, this and a warm nickel from an unhappy man. He has his way of becoming what she wants. Tugging at his sleeve, that life raft floating around his wrist, she dreams of one whole sentence spoken only to her.

It was for this she was happy. It was for something that would happen, and when that never did, it was for something else that might. It was for the clean woodwork; voices of German aunts at the head of April parades; chipped ham from the Isaly's plant around the corner, so thin you could read the newspaper through it; Sam Spade on the radio; white shirts on the line shook free of soot; it was the long attachment to the Mother of God; for something in colored windows; for one of these days; and how the silent tailor would talk of love, and if he never did, well, she knew it anyway, he loved her.

Buttons and spools, snip of the scissors on gabardine, he loved her as she kicked to the sound of the opera, to its lilt and boom, with legs too plump for the government milk that skinny Rega gets every school-day noon. The uncles give her pinches for being so round, and she is half in love with an ivory clump of needle wax, a box of cold buttons, its watery sound, all the silvery stuff of the tailor, the clear acts of stitching and assembling. From out of nowhere, there were three-piece suits.

A shaft of rose light from the leaded window of the old shop illuminated what was hers for having loved it, changing everything into pieces she could arrange and rearrange into something worth having, the way he did

98

the black scraps into a Sunday coat. She is a genius at being alone. She's dredged up buttons and wax and she is satisfied, and tells the stallions of the streetcars so, I am happy, as they pass in their rattly gallop by, while she hums to the sound of his sewing machine, and dreams, with a gift for dreaming, of foreign countries, where handsome baritone singers talk till dawn.

It was good to sit here dreaming in her father's shop, to be who she was, while the opera flowered out dark from the Philco. It was good to be plain. Adults were duty-bound to tell the absolute truth; if she was pretty they would tell her so, and when they didn't, she figured it out. Yes, it was nice to be plain. It was good to be alone.

Early morning in March of 1936, the month of the great rains, the stepmother gathered her few belongings and waded into the invisible. The rivers broke and downtown streets became canals, reflecting second- and third-story windows, submerging doorways; traffic halted and North Side houses swept by, free of their cellars; utility lines slid down from their deciduous moorings and fire rose up in a world of water; books and carpets stewed in mud. Years later the watermark still shadowed downtown buildings, and the stone of Union Trust, the Pennsylvania Railroad depot, Joseph Horne & Co. became a record of household departure, the rains, an artifact, the waters of the Ohio, the Allegheny and the Monongahela, a souvenir. Her father, unable to afford rent, moved to the back of his dwindling shop, where he slept on a black leather sofa, and the children went off to the aunts again. For two years, by trolley every Saturday, she would get back home to the bolts of cloth on Bouquet Street where this was always conversation: the fact of being in the same room.

In 1938, he plucked them from the houses of aunts and cousins and set all three atop a corner drugstore on the North Side of Pittsburgh. Hiss of the seltzer sang from silver taps. Casseroles and cakes arrived by the week, she could see them now, left by the door on the third-floor landing, wrapped in wax paper and rubber bands. When the duntes made anything, they always made it twice. For every Lord Baltimore cake made with egg yolks, a Lady Baltimore cake made from egg whites arrived on a plate; the eggs were never wasted. The fry pans, the good copper-bottom pots, and the hand sweeper made their way from Oakland. When anything was missing from their cupboards, Duntes Fritz and Simmons knew where to find it, with the kids atop the drugstore. Rega swept the rugs and frowned at dishes. As for Anna, she danced out the door to that week's courter in the Ford. She knew it then: she was pretty and had been all along, with a good head of thick brown hair; her eyes, deep-set and blue. The youngest was a newsboy at his supper, praised for his beauty, his appetite, the way he moved across a room. Her father sat nodding at their life together. He sat and nodded until the weddings, the packing plants, and the '40s shook them from his side. Except for her; no matter what, there was always room for him, no matter marriage or cramped space, she would take care of him, she would see to it.

Her girl was humming again. Best kid, Anna thought, and turned to stir the onions. The girl was watching, fascinated (she knew it) by something silly like the color of her dress or her speed at chopping and stirring, her fearlessness when it came to striking a match. She felt ridiculously tall and diminished at the same time (her children's eyes were always on her), and she was pouring out like a cup, like a pitcher, like a great river, she thought. The girl adored her and it made her nervous and fast to please. She was hard at work, and that's the way she liked it. She liked to be busy, to do what she did best.

She had an excellent inborn talent for ironing. Her sister told her so and bought her a brand-new ironing board and an immense white mangle first thing when she left her husband, more than two years ago. So she could make a living. And three new housedresses. For confidence, Rega told her, The dresses will give you confidence. She knew she had the talent, but the thought of ironing other people's shirts, the difficult cotton, the long white shirts, terrified her. She might not be good enough after all when it came to that, all those tiny pleated corners. You have more than confidence, Rega told her, You have your heritage; that's just the way it is, you're German. You can do it.

Her sister stood there in her mind with that large beautiful face like Saturn (it was planetary, orb-like, it was her older sister when you came right down to it, and it gave her confidence). Not that it was class-type work or anything, she had said to her sister at the time, but I *was* assistant hostess in my day. For fifty cents an hour at the B & G Restaurant, downtown Pittsburgh. People knew me when they came to eat; it made me feel like I owned the place. And so she promised herself right then and there, she was good enough, she would manage it.

When she got her first ironing job (even though she swore Mrs. Natali was just being kind) she was on top of the world, came running into the house to tell the kids. I got a job, I got a job. We're on top of the world, we're fine. Word would get around, she knew it. And starting with her very first pay, she saved fifty cents every week for the Mixmaster, tip-top of the line, that Rega wanted. She did it behind her back. And she'd do anything for her still. Save for luggage, save for proper silverware because Rega likes to spend a week in June on the Jersey shore and appreciates a good table. She would cat-walk on Rega's windowsills; she would do her windows. She would haul a bucket through her house and do her floors. She would make it up to her, for all the help (the house-dresses, the mangle, the secondhand furniture), for all the sad stories she didn't recognize.

A good woman is harder to find than your way to China, she always knew that. Anna Hallissey was a good woman, and no one ever wanted to let her go. Only one month after she started on her own, there was a long line to her door, even a professor from the university was in it. Twenty-one shirts a week for five dollars. It's like I'm somebody, she told Rega.

Sister Magdalena, that nice principal, knowing they were the only children in the parish school without a father at home, offered free tuition and uniforms. No one would have to know, she told her. But she was their mother, she would know. No way was anyone ever going to look at her three kids and think she couldn't give them the clothes on their backs. She was their mother; she would see to it. No way were her kids going to walk around thinking they weren't paid for in full.

Soon enough she was housecleaning for Mrs. Halloran and helping Mrs. Guntherman who cared for two old ladies across the way. She kept up the odd jobs (they didn't want to let her go) and started at East Liberty Lehmann's Department Store, at the Garden Shop in the parking lot. In less than a year she was promoted to the third floor, to the Lamps & China Department. And that little green jacket, she thought, from the Garden Shop, she no longer had to wear it; it floated off into the yard over Marie Natali's nice bushes.

Every night she stood there ironing by the kitchen door, while her children sat at the table, drawing spiders, swing sets, and eskimos, doing their problems with the chickens and apples, writing their autobiographies. They were blurry in her eye sometimes, the colors of the clothes they wore blended with the ironing stack or the pile of laundry, their faces with pages of her grocery list.

But she would stop herself right then and there. Sometimes she would make centerpieces with them for the neighbors and they would go out gathering evergreens. They made little paper graduates for those that had passed and little paper people in beds for those that were sick. It really was the last thing she wanted to do (make little paper people), it took such patience and Helen, her oldest, was very particular, it had to be done

103

just so. But she would make it up to them. The only ones in the parish school without a father, no one had to tell her that, she knew it well enough.

In the evenings when she ironed in the kitchen, sometimes her dad came out of his room and sat with them; she was glad for the company, even though it never amounted to much in the way of conversation. (He was always stitching through life in his snowy mind, she could see it happening, inside a globe all blurried with snow, he was busy making gabardine suits and winter coats.) It was best not to bother him.

Or he sat there reading history books from the high school bazaar, muttering over the censored pages of Germany. My country My country, he would say, shaking his head side to side with disbelief at even half the truth, with visions of second cousins creeping in high grass. He wiped his glasses with his stiff white handkerchief. What's the matter, Dad? And he tapped his round black shoe, once. This world . . . he said. You know . . . she said. And everybody looked.

But she would make it up to them. She would bake them a cake any minute they needed it. She would grind the cranberries (they would pop like balloons), butter-fry the onions, and the house would be flooded with love love and cooks. You know, honeybunches. She would say that to each and every one of them.

You know, she said as she stood there ironing, we're all German around here. Then she took her pinking shears to cut out words from the *Ladies' Home Journal*. To mend, to love, overcome, repair, remember, tell a friend, forgive and take two minutes to appreciate some various things. My three beautiful kids, she liked to remind them of that.

When the icebox broke down, just one month after they moved in to Dorothy Avenue, and it gave out its little whirr, That's doves, she told them. We have doves. Let me tell you about birdcall. Because there was something she wanted them to understand, some high thing they had to stand on their toes for, keep their chins up for, be brave and helpful, have hope, make an effort and put yourself out a little. She would instruct them as best she could. Love, she told them; smile every once in a while; and don't ever use your Grandpap's scissors, they're special. And remember he made those shirts you're wearing. Because Anna Hallissey was always sure to remind them of history, what was given to them, what came to them from the past. She'd tell them a story, something nice, maybe the story of the oranges that ran down the streetcar tracks on the hilly brick avenue when they were small. Your little red wagon toppled over, she told them. And the four of us went yelping, chasing the beautiful fruit back home like it was our sacred duty.

Sacred duty, she always said that, especially to her boy, These are the rules, and took him by the hand into the room he shared with her dad. I'm telling you this because I love you. These are the rules. She whispered into his hands, she shouted, she talked to him for hours. Do you see what I'm trying to tell you? and kissed his eyes. Listen to what I know. Her girls never needed to be told. They were in perfect charge of the house already at ages seven and eleven, and it really was a crime how good they were, she thought, especially the youngest. Louise

Katherine Anne Hallissey never gave her a single argument; she never wanted a single thing.

She was watching. In the cool shade under the table, onions frying in butter mixed with the clean smell of the catalog pages. With the wind from an opened window blowing the scent of onions back into the room, onions whirled in with the sweetness of carrots and white pages, and the girl's idea of summer fixed itself there in her mind. And like the swirls of women in brightly colored skirts from the pages of the catalog, the silence of the kitchen billowed out over her head, and there was no place she'd rather be than caught under the cool shade of the table, in view of a flowered skirt. But Let me help, she said, sliding the catalog and its silences aside, ready to enter some great wheel of stacked dishes, of chopped and butter-fried things.

Her mother's house began her dream of the neighborhood, her knowledge of strung cellars, plates pushed under chins, her hope of all things small and squirreled away by the doings of women, taking place all the way down the block, widening into space. From under the table she took her guess at heaven, some pure smack of it in her mother's heart, and she clung to the projects of her days, begging to help.

Sit sit, she said to her girl, who worried too much at the age of seven, she knew it, how she whirled at her skirts, wanting to help. She had always let her. She had taught her how. But she knew the girl had certain needs: to work with pegs (or had she gotten over that?), to draw in the dirt with a stick, notice an indentation of fireflies in the night. Little thing, she thought and knew it was true, because of the dot reflecting from her own blue eyeglasses.

Her birth was a terrible idea at the time, which they never should have dared to think. But there was her girl, under the table, and she dared to think it now. Someday everything will be up to you, but right now no one needs a single blessed thing, she told her.

Under the table the girl felt bereft of motion, and her mother, inarguably complete, far off, stood at the sink, chopping carrots. More than anything she knew she was alone and destined for the door, uncaptured, and returning solitary to the company of women, to a hard-built place on earth. Her mother's flowered dress was bright and hazy, her body nearly blank with sunlight. Her mother's body was thin and she knew this above all things, and could not look at her without seeing something so light and strong that it flew, or hovered, would not touch down but whirled overhead, unreachable, like a sorrow or thought capable of itself.

Sacred duty, she thought. She stood at the sink and could feel it all around her like the wings of a fly, it was buzzing. There was anger in the scrub rags, limitation in the rungs of chairs. The corners of the sofa were hopeless after all, crumbed with lint. And in the whirl of the vacuum suddenly ending, there was only back and forth, the uphill downhill of everything. So they teach you ABC, she thought: This is A, this is B, this is C. But why no gobbledygook letter in between? Why just do your sacred

107

duty till you die? When you start to question, no one's more amazed than you. Years later, she would tell that to her girl. Blind obedience is sad, she'd tell her. It stops you from having vision, even a vision that you could go to town by yourself.

Across the years sometimes when her mother didn't know, the girl would stand in doorways and watch her from across the room, and imagine who she was, sitting at her desk in half-light, writing letters to aunts and cousins, as the soft large loops of her alphabet made her arm swing into air. Round and clean, I have a beautiful hand, her mother would say, and seeing her there, she would show her how to do it, like this. The Catholic Church did great things for my penmanship, Anna would laugh, but they ruined my mind. Sometimes the phone would ring, and her mother's body wouldn't budge an inch, her hand enjoying its flourish in air. The phone rang until it stopped.

Sometimes there's just nothing you need to hear, her mother would tell her. There are things you needn't bother with, Lulie Hallissey. Sometimes there's nothing you need to do but live.

Now the silence of the kitchen billowed out above her head, her childhood stretched before her, flat and sunlit, for one moment insinuating forever, and under the table her small body lived its large space, with no mother, no father, only the summer yards, their green presence behind the house, where she would not yet go.

Under the Table

Louise, 1955–1967

Life Before with Tumbledown Dad

🖐 Hard snow rims the rims of my black boots.　🖐

I stand in the kitchen. In from the yard where the snow hills up pushing against the uneven planks of the fence, where the blackbird lands on a splintery edge, brittle-toed and poking up, I stand in the kitchen, stuffed with clothes.

The sudden moment of the house stings the tips of my face. I stand here waiting heavy as wet wood, the kitchen is heavy with lemons, my coat smelling of tea.

Just a little vinegar, nothing simpler, calls Mum. So what do we need in pickling? says Dad, rooting through the bottles behind the cellar door.

Hard snow rims the rims of my black boots. Mummy rushes to me like a thin blue train, chugging, and kisses me, chugging. Her hands tug stiff mittens from the mechanical ends of my arms that work in vertical cracks of air.

Rounded now with the shape of my hands they lie on the high painted radiator, bumpy with ice, where tiny hairs of wool poke up, silver bugs of snow. The shape of my hands melts on the radiator in the curvy waves of heat by the window.

The ends of my arms are far off at the beginning of a bucket. I cart snow. My hands blinded by mittens. From here to there, slapping down the snow, covering color. Out back I cart snow heavy in the metal pink bucket, packed tight like the soul in the body. It is buried now, abandoned there and silent till spring, when it pops up a dusty red. A dumped weight then I lie on my lost back, signaling angels into the snow, spreading my arms to the wings, my legs to the dresses of angels. I lie on my back with my mouth sprung open tasting the tiny metals of snow. This is the reason I have worked so hard, thick with clothes, with stinging feet and cheeks, for this moment, the whole world leafing with snow. I am listening now and this is not silence. The ground rings like me in my ears.

Gangway! says Dad and the blackbird scatters from its fence with the explosion of my father into the room. So what do we need in pickling?

Stories are less than sound itself as it springs from here. My father springs from behind the cellar door, and he, like the whole of childhood, which leaves me and does not leave me, like a sound in a net, will never be told better than this: one-handed, the crack of an egg at the edge of a thick-rimmed bowl; from the roof's tarred edge, the plop of ice caught in round snow; and underfoot the cold snap of a branch blown windward, scratching across cleared sidewalks; storm doors and kettles; the rum of metal; the bump bum bum on brick; the big fussing of wings; hands running through the bells of the vinegar bottles.

Gangway! says Dad.

So where's the vinegar, he says, in all this damned rigmarole. His hands are blind.

My throat hurts, I tell her. When I hear Dad's voice that means my throat hurts. That means I go to bed. I like to go. I like lids and spoons, paper, pots, rags that are old and very friendly, but bed best of all. I don't know much of anything but lids and spoons and rags.

I hate noise. I get tapped to sleep. I put rags over everybody in the kitchen. I leave them behind but then they rumble in. Eddy climbs in beside me. He smells like Shredded Wheat. His forehead shines like a spoon. I use his arm around my head for darkness. I put his arm over my eyes and ears. My father is humming deep inside himself, there is a waltz in his big black shoes.

Daddy waltzes Helen across the tabletop, I look. There they are waltzing. Helen's in her nightgown dancing across the tabletop. His suspenders swing at this sides. Daddy loves his arms when sister's in them. When the dance slows down, Daddy sings low and his kisses tip tip on the wall. Mum smiles. Helen is a quiet sack. She's lifted. Like a ribbon over his shoulder.

Potatoes for sale, Potatoes for sale, Daddy calls out, lonely in the dark.

Helen's hair is gold and good to have around you. Her hair swings, and Mum touches it as it touches Dad. They set my sister down. She's the older sister with her own bed. Croon croon, Little Darlin', says Dad.

And switches on the light. Light goes down again because Eddy wears his Cassidy hat to bed and I put my eyes under its brim. My mouth sags open. My mouth looks into his face. Mum and Dad sink low into sheets like boats into water, like little dark nests, they fall away, into the river under the bed. I keep my hands. Near Eddy. Near Buddy. I call my brother Buddy. Hey sister, Oh brother. And the night shuts down.

It is sizzling.

Someone pours Coca-Cola for a nickel from a cracked blue pitcher. Daddy sits at the edge of the bed in the middle of the night and cries. Trot trot trot, he says from deep inside himself. There are just too many of you, says Daddy. There are too many out there.

Falling apart, says Mum. Mum says she is falling apart. There's nothing wrong with me, says Dad, It's you. You're just a little dizzy in the bughouse.

Someone pours Coca-Cola and I wake up to tap tap tap on my arm which is all mixed up with Eddy's leg. Eddy's hat is on his foot. I put my eyes under its brim. I like his hat and his hat likes me. I give a kiss to his hat. Dad with a sweep swings the hat up, slams it on his own head, laugh laugh. Eddy uses my arm for silence. He wraps my arm around his ears. Daddy taps on mine, my ears. Wants to know if we'll be here when he gets back.

114

He smells like toast. I want some. I tell him so. He says, Will you be here when your Daddy gets back? He says, tap tap tap, little girl. Mummy comes in, says, Let them sleep. Laugh laugh, says Dad, who sings out loud about fences. Says not to put him there, let him roam roam roam. Paris too, he says. Meaning nothing. For no reason. I want toast.

So where's Daddy? He's in Distress. He's buying ham. Give a wave to your daddy at the window. He'll be right back.

His sleeves taste bitter like dandelions. When his eyes say okay, I get on his lap because it is. Then he lifts a spoon to my mouth. Then he lifts a spoon to my mouth. This once.

Once he went away and bought ham for a whole year or ten days and maybe I like this, but Mummy shouts, slapping meat into the icebox.

So where's Dad?

He's in Distress, Mother said. Daddy's gone to a town called Distress. Somewhere nearby.

Mummy hurries us up. Everybody runs but I get pulled. Then we're all in water. Then we're all in clothes. Mine are still hot from Mummy's iron. We stand in a line by the door; she pats us into place. I hold on to the bottom of my dress. I squinch it up in my fist and give it a toss to Eddy. It used to be his when he was a little girl. He won't catch. Mum says, Don't don't, your daddy's coming home. She straightens it out, her hand like an iron but cool and skinny.

115

There's Dad's whistle and we all scoot. Them to him, me to the underneath of the table where I find things out. I look for reasons in people's eyes or in their feet. Kiddos, says Dad and rushes into the kitchen like a big fat train where I already am. I tap on knees and get hauled out by the elbow. I am raised up on telephone books that wobble under me, slipping.

Dad smiles, at himself, I think. Easy street, he says. Guess what? So okay, here's a game. What? Says he got promoted. Big hot shot now, he says. He's a big deal. Mum hurrahs. Her pink glasses tilt when her kisses snap on his hands. Then he puts his hands like two white fish in the middle of his plate. What's in it for me? he says.

What's wrong? What's the matter?

Dad stands all day in one spot and sings in his paper hat. Now he's promoted. Says he has to boss people around. I can't handle it, says Dad, I'm over my head. The chips are flying, Thy will be done. Try try try again if at first you don't. And then he laughs. Just be me and get a penny for it, he says, and gives Eddy a slap on the back. Sink or swim buster and Eddy laughs. So okay. But Helen doesn't. Why?

I'm gagging, Daddy.

He hums and eats then hits her plate with his spoon, his mouth curvy as a cloud, an old root. Till Kingdom come you'll sit there at my supper table and finish those goddamned peas. Let her go, says Mummy who's making a mountain out of a molehill, says Dad.

Mummy wants to know why he talks that way. Clichés, she tells him. She thinks he should read more, it might relax him. He says that's rubbish, she says that's

116

bliss. That's waste, he says, he has no time to relax. There's too many of you, says Dad. I can't handle it. Mummy says, Yes you can you're doing fine. He twists his sleeve tight around the white neck of his hand. Then he's fine. She gives him a kiss. He's handsome. Let's not and say we did, says Dad.

What's the matter? What's wrong?

Everybody has a book except Daddy and the dishes are done. Daddy's a handsome old devil, or so he says. He hides behind the red sofa, looking out. He's looking out at Mummy who reads on the porch swing while it rains, wrapped up in a little pink cloud called peace, called poetry on the porch. Poetry is bliss, says Mummy, especially when it rains.

I scoot behind a wall to watch Dad hide. He pokes his curly head up. Dad is tap tap tap on the glass. There's Mum's head turning but Dad scoots down. I scoot behind. So okay. We are playing a game with Mum. There's Mum's head at peace again. Then Daddy behind the sofa is tap tap tap again. His white knuckles flutter against the window of my mother's hair. Her head turns to nobody there. Mum squints into the glass. Dad pops up and slaps. He slaps his hand full against the window of Mummy's face. Dad ducks and laughs. I scoot behind.

Daddy gets out the door. Now he's whispering, now he's screaming on the porch that poetry is a business for no-goods. Highfalutin nonsense for bleeding hearts; we can't afford it; so just go ahead and pitch it; pitch the rubbish, all your high ideas. The books go sailing down into the alley, pages spread like white birds' wings. Mummy clatters down the steps in a hush of rain-soaked pages and stoops down in the street. Dad leans over the banister. I want everybody out of here by tomorrow, says Dad.

Daddy runs out and comes back with an icebox. Brand-new Kelvinator, he says. I stand and watch it. It watches me. The Zenith arrives to a line of neighbors waving reverently from their front porches. Mum is in the next room, asking why. A bird in the hand is worth three in the bush, says Dad. Mum says she's going to get a job. Dad says No. Mum says Yes. She wants to help. Dad says No. Mummy says Must.

My mother works at a drugstore, a job for a slouch and a no-good, says Dad. He rushes home from work and honks the horn, says What a fine fandango this is, forward all, when the sun goes down. We put Mummy in a drugstore, then drive back home with Daddy who finds a bump in the road, says it's a rolly coaster in the hills of Pittsburgh, forward ho.

We sit around the house with Dad, chafing at the bit, he says. He tells us stories of God and toads. Words are jokes he plays on us. Rosenbergs, he says, for nothing, no reason. We wait and make mistakes. Put up your dukes, he says. Never say die.

Our mother walks into the living room and wants to know what's going on, her eyes a pale sharp blue. Why aren't they in bed? They should be in bed by now.

Our father wraps his arms around his head. I pull at his sleeves until he comes undone. Don't bend the tin,

Don't touch the merchandise, he says, You're driving me crazy. Dad says we drive him buggy. Mummy says it's life. That's life. So Mummy comes home and stays there.

When Mummy wants to know what's going on, I tell her my throat hurts. She hides me in her lap where I know nothing, and kisses me. You're a strong, healthy girl. We are all strong, healthy people around here.

She rattles the Pittsburgh *Press* around my head. Then Daddy swipes the newspaper, says, Don't be a no-do, where's food? Then he laughs, goes off to hammer at something real. I climb down to see.

He's making little chairs. He likes to do that for us. He's pasting on little pictures of blue and pink puppies in suits and ties, having tea. Listen to me, says Daddy. Wide-eyed, he stands up curved, sleek as a cat in his gangster pose, leans against the doorway, his feet crossed at the ankles, arms folded across his chest, eyes lowered and to the side. We're all in the same boat around here. And remember, he says, you need me.

I climb back into Mummy's lap. Mum looks up at him. He looks down at Mum. Dummkopf, he says. Ha ha, I love it when you look so worried. And you, says Dad to someone behind me, have holes in your head. I sit on my hands and close my eyes, I won't look at him, never will, not completely, not once, in his eyes, in his whole life. I am falling asleep.

I am falling deep without weight asleep in my mother's lap, and lifted high, am only a distance that stretches head to foot. She touches my head and my head is real but apple-size. My heart is also like an apple, ripe

119

on its branch within my smallest body. When she is near me, I am weighed down. My heart is an apple.

I am falling from the tips of her hands into the covers, I am set down into the warm milky smell of my brother beside me again. Eddy puts his hat on my fist. He puts his hand under the hat with mine and says, Fine fandango, and I giggle.

No more valentines for Daddy.

When he croons all boozy and pretend like Dean Martin, Mummy packs us into bed with a holler, snapping out the lights.

Helen climbs chairs. Helen hides knives on top of the refrigerator behind the Magnavox in the middle of the night, and makes me hold her feet. We hide knives behind the Magnavox because my sister says Daddy will make Mummy go to jail when she kills him.

Mummy's on the floor and can't get up. She wants a glass of water. My sister runs to get a glass of water for Mummy, golden haired and on her toes at the sink. She runs to Mummy, she is dancing now, she is singing the alphabet, Aah she starts and turns, she runs to Dad, pitches it at him. Right in his face. Mother's dead, she says, and gets smacked.

Mummy rises, says That's it. That does it, says Mummy, once a child gets touched.

We stand by the door with our shopping bags. Don't I get a valentine? asks Daddy. That's it, says Mummy, once the children get involved. Look at that new sofa, says Dad, doesn't that deserve a valentine? He wants to know. Eddy wants to answer. Buddy wants to answer. I call my brother Buddy. Daddy cries in the armchair, says he needs a valentine and a chance. Poor bad Daddy. Nobody answers. We just sail out the door. Buddy.

I get older and come away with nothing, but my voice is God's magician. Voice knows things in the shape of a rumble, in the dark inside a hat, in bells of vinegar bottles, in the taste of a cotton dress. All progress will depend on it, to unravel the years, bared to the taste of a cotton dress. Voice is a complete life I will never have some day, but it will move me toward itself, and from these small things, I will people the house that has wandered away from me.

River has a voice and I do too; from the very first day I've been hearing. And although I am stranded here in my unextraordinary childhood, low to the floor, in a shaft of sunlight, simple as a bead, all along it's lap lap lap with a voice underneath that knows things.

My voice is like a river. It will rise.

The Second House, 1955

⌂ Mummy gives us cold cut apples from the cellar. ⌂
When she goes alone to the cellar I drop everything,
I go to the top of the dark and put my feet on my hands.
Hush says Mum and before she goes gives me a seashell
and a soup ladle to hear the little parts of God and
Atlantic City. Listen to the nice horses, says Mum. She
goes down the soft damp wood of the stairs and the little
horses of sound go with her. Her blue glasses, flared at
the tips and tipped with metal, make notches of light on
the stairwell. Her feet scatter down the stairs.

My mother is afraid of the dark. She runs through
the cellar, thudding through the baskets, then back up
again into sunlight with a skirtful of apples.

The knife snaps on the countertop and apples break
open with a slap.

My father used to stare like the winter apple with its tight brown eyes in a face of snow.

My mother's body wipes the window glass with its yellow dress. When the end of her dress swings up to her mouth I put my face on the cold heads of her knees. Sweet warm baby, says Mum.

The thick turned hem of her dress with its long striding stitches falls down damp to my face with the tin smell of the window dirt. I stand inside the edges of her yellow dress. Her dress lights up around me.

Childhood is a shady place except for my mother's dress. The taste of it is winter thin and soapy.

When I come out from under the tip of her dress, her hand comes down with a white cut apple. I eat the touches of green. When she puts her thumb to her mouth and at the corner of mine presses a wet half moon, little green pieces of the apple fall to the floor, in a tiny crush of sweetness, are gone under my shoe.

House rings with the newness of its echoes. Rain in the gutter. Spoon against the coffee tin. My mother cracks a spoon against the coffee tin. Its sound echoes in the bare kitchen, through the gray foyer, up the stairs to apartments 2 and 3 on Dorothy Avenue, and echoes in the miles of the city through wet and tire-crossed streets.

Cold seeps in through the window cracks from the high green of yard, wild with winter grass and weeds shoulder-tall to a girl. It is in the back of our minds, the too-large yard where we do not want to go. The weather is like strands of hair.

123

Winter makes the house large, the rooms are big with drafts. We are lost in house.

When the furnace kicks on, warming the hollow cupboards, steam hisses up through white pipes, a gift from the landlord. We are held tight now, gobbling apples, caught in a strange sunlight from dark clouds. Groceries lie jumbled in bags, where cold cans grow warm in winter sunlight that has come so far across the rainy city.

Mummy's tired. She is hot and bright in the yellow kitchen but her skin on her knees and her thumb is cold. My blue glasses stare at her, her body, its brightness and its little bones at the wrists. She is packing in the groceries, she is rushing now from cupboards to closets, vanished to the thin shelves along the stairwell.

I bear down into my shoes, with my arms and legs, their simple weight. This satisfies me, this solitary stand of my own, and to be this little. I should be this little, carted here and there, tended in my simple weight.

Which becomes immense. And this also satisfies. This being not weight but becoming light, this not laughing but being thoughtful, becoming busy, sorrowful, being not skin but becoming good. I should be lifted from her, from her wavering. With my narrow arms, with my still legs, with my lips that do not eat too much, from my hunger and cold, from my heat and motion, from my own existence, I should save her. It pains her when I sneeze.

Outside a car whizzes by. My mother appears in sunlight like a windy thing in her too-large dress. A car whizzes by through wet streets, and from the rivers rising and from the clouds' descent, my father's hair is soaked with rain.

Gloomy, says Mum. Don't be so. Don't be so gloomy. This is our lucky day in February.

Why this is our lucky day, she says, rooting through a suitcase filled with waves of colored paper, her hands deep in knotted ribbons.

My mother takes paper hearts from the plaid bottom of the suitcase and tapes them to the wall in a design like flight. She is rushing now, she is scattering. Whether she meant it that way or not.

It is birds.

I keep my eyes on the ground deep inside of house. From a small allowance in the eye I follow Mummy's brown laced shoes into tight rolls of damp clothes in a pink plastic bushel. She stands there ironing, I pray for her legs. I sit watching from the sofa where nothing is ever my fault again. I dangle my legs and twist. The rough green sofa leaves the imprint of flowers on the backs of my knees. In charge of everything, I narrow my eyes. I curl into the cracks of the sofa, into the sleepy heat of the iron and the hazy hiss of the mangle on the immense white shirts.

I never count to seven and minus things because I don't know how. I plan for picnics under green skies while Helen counts my money. We are saving for birthday, for Mummy's green radio. House collects my dreams skyward in the attic, where I believe in Heaven, under its pointed roof.

Our lives blow through the folds of her skirt.

125

We go where we want. We are little, unsettled. Gobbling apples.

My mother snaps a white shirt into air and the smell of starch billows out into the room. And already I know the smell of her new hands afterward, changed by the starch, bittered, reddened.

Cat looks. I talk to Cat and listen all the while except to say Hey Cat, who is the color of her hair. And that is the famous talk with Cat in the world.

My eyes are skimming over the arms of the sofa, over just their very edges which are very thin. I am not wholly present through the hours of our ironing, no not completely, except there is a warm salvation in the smell of the starch, the determined snap of the shirt, the heat of the iron, the taste of her dress, and in the rest of these things like the sofa, which is green. And when I look, you think that this is what I see. But this is not what I see. This is not what I hear at all.

Here with the knickknacks deep inside of house, where everything is something I can ruin, I know pure boredom in the silence I accomplish here. The silence I accomplish here to find I am alive in a shaft of sunlight comes with me. And what I see is what lies behind me, like the rain-soaked streets, large feet stamping in their shoes, a doorstep dampened at the edges. This is where I grieve, though I do not know this, it is only mud level, it is only slightly ruined, and I like this where I am.

Mr. Ellis, the bachelor with the yellow hair, a professor from the university, comes stooped and sorry through the front door. Poking in his toes, letting in the cold, he is sorry for the big number of his shirts stiff and perfect on their wire hangers at the top of the door.

This is my oldest, says Mum, my son and my baby. Nine, six, and five, she says, counting us like Guy Lombardo.

So that's your baby the people always say, and my face drifts up like a balloon from the pillow's crack. I go where I can in my smallness and I am counted, smiling, shimmering against the wall. Mr. Ellis bends to my smallness, his hands on his knees. So this is your baby. Like curls of apple peel, little parts of me fall away with no sound to the floor.

But sister smirks, bobs like a bird walk, once, her round pink face into mine. Bay-bee, she says. Her mouth sings the alphabet into my eyes. Aah Bay Bee. When mother throws an idle arm around my ducked head, brother jumps like a rubber band into the sofa beside me. He shimmers, funny as string, skinny as a crack of door light. I am inches and warm in the floating fort of their bodies. And for one single second, somebody forgot to put anyone on this earth but baybee.

Then that's done with and everything is just bing bing bing down the line. Then they put these fish in cans and everything gets too close. Sardines, my mother says. So okay. Usually the days go unexplained and you get carted from one thing to the next.

Fort Pitt, Mummy says, I quit. Then she sets down the iron in a bright slam of triumph. Fort Pitt, that's it.

An empty holster swings around my hips. Black with silver tacks, and too big, it shifts to the rear. I will not

127

wash my hair. I stand with my mother on the gray porch, waving good-bye. My hair is damp oily strings and I will not wash it. It is flat on my head as many as grass. I am plain and I long for the lost sofa and my presence that sits there waiting to be forgiven. Behind me is the wet doorstep, one room that has become another, streets that are now other streets, where I am still running in the presence of a wish. I wish to be forgiven. I go here and there uncaught.

She watches the shirts go like children, tossed into the back seat in a stiff white heap, and her heart sinks just a little. She is sad now and we are at home in her sadness, in its very familiar; we are little, we settle in. Mr. Ellis is on the go. He tosses the shirts like children in a stiff white heap and they rumple. It took me a good half hour to do just one shirt, she says. Loose at her side the five-dollar bill waves in Mum's hot white hand. It is a poor strong hand bumpy with good blue veins. I see that it is hers and I fit myself beneath it.

I see all things that are hers like her hair, which is thick and forest brown, dreamy with waves. I see my own bare legs, which I have made bare against her wishes because it was hot in sunlight and in the ironing. I see bare legs as if these too were hers, more than just born of her but walking her steps, trying to match their music, catching up through race and marvelous balance, my own sheer breathless effort. My achievement, I am hers. I stand still beside her, racing, nesting into her. I am racing upward, climbing her, scrambling for my place. She is staggering under my weight, under my intentions.

My skin makes Mummy shiver. Her hand is dangling at her side. I fit myself beneath it, where I am skimmed like a pond. I am skimmed like a pond for just minutes.

It is growing dark and I am tight in my clothes again. I follow her brown laced shoes into the drops of rain at the edge of the porch. And just like when a leaf is dragged across the porch and, in a sudden arc of wind, touches her, I ask: Can I come, too? And she lets me.

Walking down the block through the rain-soaked neighborhood, my mother is a radio. Black wires bobbing in wind glisten with beads of water, with the electricity of sound, she is singing. I bow my heart three times everywhere in the presence of the Lord. I take her fast steps fast.

You know, child, she tells me, it's like I'm laughing at everybody because I'm out here having a good time and they're all locked up inside but I'm out here laughing. So I say: Me too, Mum. Me too.

And my father's hair is soaked with rain.

Under the Table

🖊 Right now I'm under the table hiding. People say 🖊 I color pretty good and even well, and no one's ever going to make me go outside these lines.

I watch my mother's laced white shoes with slanted heels, bent at the tips of her toes. Rounded, they ratatat across the floor, from here to there so quick, I can't keep up or speak.

This is not my house. I'm in my mother's place of employment, at least one of them, in the house next door on Dorothy Avenue, in the very residence of Miss Mary Louise Sims and her little sister, Anne Cecile, who are, and I'm telling the truth, 100 years of age, and 89.

Right now they're asleep, side by side, in their mechanical beds with silver wheels deep in Ali Baba carpets, in the dayroom papered pink, because it's ohsopleasant, says Mrs. Guntherman, the nurse, who moved in and put them there, to spare us all the steps, smack in the middle of the parlor, which is what Miss Mary Louise calls it. Why am I sleeping in the parlor? she'd like to know at least fifty times a day. My guests will think it strange.

That's me, kind of, the guest. I visit the sisters at a distance from under the mahogany every Saturday. Sun's good for your blood, says Mrs. Guntherman, and pats their beds when they complain.

Shy and made of tinsel, they sniff the air and give a little shiver. Like fish out of water, Mum says to herself. She shakes her head and sighs. Her heavy eyelids close and flutter open. Then lifting her skirt above the knees, she breaks into a tiny run up steps, her feet softly drumming ratatat. In the folds of her skirt she sneaks down evidence of their rooms upstairs and pats it into their hands: a doily sachet in the shape of a human face stuffed with crumpled petals; a red Excelsior Diary from 1882 (which all it says is *Very Pleasant Day, Pleasant Day, Stormy Day, Very Pleasant Day,* and that's the way it was, honest to God, in Pittsburgh, in 1882); one whole hatbox of china rosettes of no purpose on earth whatsoever, except they exist and were made by their father who spent a lifetime shaping them, baking them, which is not the worst a man can do, my mother says, rosettes. Then she puts everything back into tissue while the ladies smile into space, and sleep.

Lordy, says Miss Cecile. Oh Lordy, help me, Mrs. Hallissey. My mother, who comes here every Saturday, cranks the bed and the bed cranks up. She bends over the body of Miss Anne Cecile, wraps an arm around the back of her neck, the arm of Miss Anne Cecile, it hangs there, surprised, like a starched ribbon. Hold tight, Mum says, fishing her out from under slipped sheets, sliding her arms under Miss Cecile's white dolly head knees, little tender eggs, then heaves, the body of Miss Anne Cecile, placing it by the window in a chair with clawed feet. It will walk away with Miss Anne Cecile very soon.

The only traveling they ever do is from being lifted by my mother from one spot of the bed to another (Miss Louise) or to the window (she prefers it, Miss Cecile).

My mother's body is stranded in the sun like a schoolgirl, lost in the huge parlor. Her fingers scissor a clump of housedress when tiny Miss Louise, drowning in waves of sheets made sharp from knuckles and knees, raises her hand from under the covers, pokes up her head with white ruffled feathers for hair, narrows the already narrow slits of her eyes, and points her crooked finger at me every time I'm here, What's that? What is she doing in my residence?

Why, that's my little girl, says Mum, that's Lulie Hallissey, my daughter. Don't you remember?

And that's the only reason I come here in the first place. Because I know I get to hear my mum say such a nice thing about me right in front of my face. Yessiree Bob, that's my little girl. And I can't help but know I'm guilty of that.

Lordy, says Miss Louise, who has my name. Mum fetches the bedpan; I study the dust that speckles the air. Dust is from the old ones, the quiet ones, it's their ancient feathers, it comes from the down on their cheeks, from the tops of their heads and the backs of their knees. So that's dust. It's from baby ones, the noisy ones, it's the down on my arms, it's my feathers falling from the backs of my knees.

I lie here under the table, flat on my back past lunchtime, counting Mummy's sorrows. Sorrow of the pork bone, sorrow of the brown banana, broken yolk, sorrow in the track of the worm in the soft peach that I pitch to the ceiling, Holy Moses, and she will catch it and eat it, the sorrow of the meal is hers. Umm Umm, she says, nothing wrong with it, stony bread.

That's why I make sure she gets her orange juice. Only if you are a kid or a grandpap are you allowed one itty glass a day because that's all Mummy has the money for. It hurts to drink it, so I chase at her heels, I hate juice, I tell her. I set it on the bathroom sink, on the bureau, in her flat shoe, just to let her know I'm serious, until finally she says all right. All right child, my sweetest baby, and drinks the juice.

I can afford to do without a lot of things because I am a strong, healthy girl in Our Lord, because my scapular verifies my apostleship in league with the Sacred Heart of Jesus bow your head, and because I have the body of a boy. Besides, it's my sacred duty to get to Heaven. Everyone in Heaven is a famous person. My mother will be famous someday. In my mind I always go to Purgatory. But I am in the line that gets to God, and someday I will matter. And I know it is my sacred duty to sing songs, to protect my books from snow and rain, because books like songs are sacred. Work is sacred. Knickknacks are sacred. And the rules. It's the worst sin in the world not to hear the rules or your true vocation, like nun nun nun late at night in your ear. Already I know I have to be a nun, not that I want to, because nearly every last dumb girl has to be one, wear black nightgowns, get plenty of soap, because everybody knows soap is the thing to give them and they will always take it, the nuns.

Sacred duty, says Mum. And I learn what that means from under the table at Mrs. Halloran's house too, where we go once a month on Mum's day off from her job at the department store. Last month when our oven blew up on her arm, she went on working at Mrs. Halloran's house with one arm tucked behind her back, because work is the thing you do and get done. Burned arm or no, Mrs. Halloran's mattresses need air.

    I run through leafy Shadyside streets to Mrs. Halloran's at lunch hour and climb the stairs to the stripped rooms upstairs, determined to be her other arm, and together we flip them over. Right then and there she teaches me how to make hospital corners on beds because it makes the world much nicer. There now, isn't that nice? she says, tucking in the sheet, giving it a sharp final tug. Doesn't that make the world much nicer? She looks up at me then from the tucked corner of the bed and I see that it is her, with eyes a papery blue, overlarge like Heaven, and I see there is a movie star in the dark waves of her hair, behind her glasses, in the full turns of her skirt, where she hides her hands, though I see.

    Nicked by walls, by the flaws in the woodwork, by floorboard nails hidden in the colors of the varnish, bitten red from bleach and smoking buckets of hot gray water that warm my face, they twist the colored clothes, wring mops. They spread me back and send me off. Because of what I see, I do not need a single thing to eat or soothe me. They hush me down. They are God's. They rest at the center of my silence. They send me off, into an urgent need, into another, not myself, whose hands are soft now and pudgy and will not take a single thing too easily.

Let's go, says Mum. I'm hiding under the dining room table again because Mrs. Halloran's children have come home for lunch. What gets me here is shame; just because my mother cleans their floors suddenly I am the daughter of the cleaning lady, Mrs. Hallissey, and this is not true; I am the daughter of my mother. She takes me by the hand and turns me to her in the hallway. You have to have spirit where your job's concerned. Work is like religion, she says, Sure you don't know God, but like the song says, the Spirit moves ya anyhow. Keep your chin up, child, you have a beautiful face. God gave us English, use it and speak up. And against my will, I am raised high when I see her face, suddenly I believe in everything, in birdsong, in shine of the linoleum, in conversation. So what's new at your private school, I ask the children. Then slump my eyes at them.

Now Eddy and me bring home the gambling boys. We linger by the ironing board, begging her with shut eyes to show her muscle. We're betting quarters that she can ring the bell at Kennywood Park and get us cigars or win us a turquoise teapot. After a lot of pleading, she blushes, she rolls her sleeve and there it is, all white and bluey. We hoot and holler and smack our foreheads. And the gambling boys shout, Hey, Mrs. Hallissey!

Because of Mummy's work, we live among pictures of Rolling Rock horses, paintings of Paris ladies, centerpieces on the blond buffet, and rows of books, their edges gilded lavender and blue. Our flowered drapes are tailormade because of the kindness of our landlord. Once a month he huffs and waddles in. Everything fine everything fine, he nods and nods and listens to any sorrow we might have, like rain in the cellar. Then his redheaded girlfriend, Dearie, tall and French in a black beret, takes it all down in a steno pad and smiles at me like we were related. I rush to the door when Dearie comes in, I am nearly tumbled into her long black skirt, though I have absolutely everything I need, which anybody knows if they've ever tried to give me anything.

Once a year we wash the walls within height, and every other month, all the windows, in and out; we tend peach, pine and apple trees; set bricks on the diagonal, completing a garden; Mummy fixes the back door, she fiddles with the screws and teaches me hammers and drivers and brads; every summer we haul the glider from the cellar and set out the pillows, ooph, we sit down; she jumps up, she wipes the stairs and windowsills; she cooks us a good dinner; Go lie down, she tells us, you're straining.

Then she bakes the cookies. I sell them for the babies. Babies in alleys or India, with no mother and no father, they are screaming in their beds, they are missing parts of their faces, they have no windows or relations, and never even heard of Jesus. I want to bring one home and raise it myself, give it little hoops and stew. I hate stew.

Then she helps me decorate my collection can with flowers because it's extra nice to do it that way. Now I can go to the best places she says, the Salon de Beauté, the expensive butcher's, and ask, Will you give a nickel for the babies? Then I bite my hand until they do. If you give a nickel you can get the babies their very own bowl, the word of our Lord, and a doctor, all for a nickel, I tell the people.

If I'm not busy buying babies, I'm hiding from Russia. At Mercy School we are filing off to the cellar for air raid drills, we are falling with shut eyes under our desks. We can not look out the window, we will melt. We will be alive tomorrow; that is only a rumor. And all we really want in this world is to go home and die with our mothers, to kiss them one last time.

But you must not love your mother more than God, they tell me. You must sacrifice your mother to the Cross. And though dashed onto earth with her, Heaven is your one and only home.

I'm always just about to lose everything I have on earth, but I never do because I whisper to the holy men. People like Jesus come to see me past midnight. I get old old old with laces on my head, loiter under pictures of the Sacred Heart, and I sleep with the Infant of Prague.

I put my arm around its five-inch body, place its crowned head on my pillow. Once when its starched lace sleeves and neck ruff cut my hand, I woke up bleeding and swore it was the stigmata; I prayed that it was. Now Mummy forbids me to sleep with the Infant of Prague one more night. My bed's already crowded with angels, and sometimes I see the tiny smoky face of Jesus or the crown of thorns floating headless on the wall. Underneath my bed I keep my collection of laminated holy cards from Sister Magdalena and a flashlight. St. Christina and St. Joan in orange and silver flames, handsome Sebastian with the arrows in his side. All of the saints have locked themselves in their rooms. They are lying under their beds in the darkness. They wear the bristles of animals under their plain soft dresses, and smile.

Meanwhile, Get some sun, says Mum. But I stay put, in a heap of crayons and books under the table. I love the tales of Davy Crockett whose cradle was a snapping turtle, and I love Joe Magarac, the Steel Man, who melted himself to save others. I love Paul Bunyan, covered wagons, rabbit pictures, Zorro, and kittens who wear britches. All of my heroes are either men or baby animals, except for the Blessed Mother who is my best friend.

Dear Blessed Mother

I love You Blessed Mother I love you I do so Please do not cry becosea I love You and Please do not feall sad becosea I will sheer You up with sacrifices and hugs and kisses for You and Your Sweet Jesuses.

Sun, my mother says.

On a windless day, my mum and I hang laundry, bing bing bing in magnificent order. Hush hush hush on the line, like a string of sounds we didn't say. The sheet.

This is very big. Mum disappears into it, taking its great width across her body. Her chin comes back, holding it. Her spread arms work and diminish it. Scattering myself at its edges near the grass, desperate to catch what never falls, I land on my bent toes. I leap toward the sound of it, Here, let me help.

Today I have done everything wrong and she has done it over, talking me through it. Nicely, she says, Like this, Bing bing bing, Towels together, Panties together, Shirts by the shoulder all together, Two pins each. I dumped the lugged bushel of wet things on the line, while she swept black water in the cellar; Hey surprise, and in my hurry, all cockeyed, bedlam on the line, fever in the heart. What's next?

Why not get some sun, she says. Your daddy's on his way. But I never want to go. Because.

Wildcat of the dad roars up to the curb, the Chrysler door swings open, and his voice rolls out like a whale. What's the matter, says Dad, Got cotton in your ears? We jump in quick before he gets out and into our kitchen. His voice struts like a marching band with his big talk in the front car seat, with his twenty reasons why he's late or wasn't here yesterday. Helen gets red in the face, tightens her fists, You're a liar, she says, and then he sings. He thinks he is the only one here. He talks to the windshield how we must never disobey or tell lies, especially to your father, the one he is pretending to be. Your daddy, he says of some other man he lost, is gonna give you a lickin' if you don't tell the truth. We shrug our shoulders, snap our lips shut. Your ole daddy, he says, eyeing the windows of our house, knows what he's talking about. I said your Mum's malarkey. No buts about it.

We shiver in sunlight; we long for the road when the wind takes over. Somewhere in us, we recognize our father's voice from the phone calls in the middle of the night. Tell your mother she's a bitch. And somewhere in us we remember the phone calls from That poor lady again, Mum says. Where's your Dad? she wants to know—and our mother takes the phone and tells her, Hush, it will be all right, I'll tell him to call you. It is hazy here where heat and sunlight ripple the windshield. We are still idling at the curb, shivering to go fast. When will Daddy start this car?

We roll past the Natalis' neat red brick at the corner; its kingdom of trimmed hedges and sloping lawn is the last familiar we see. We roll past Shadyside, through East Liberty streets, onto Liberty Avenue past blurry store-fronts in a tangle of speed and stoplights. We roar into the otherwise unseen, into the darker light of Bloomfield, its houses smaller, tighter, in rows with no porches, into secret alleys. He has no money for ice cream. Your Daddy just made a car payment; no dough for ice cream, maybe cherry pop.

Daddy has to go see a man about a horse. We wait as long as we can in sunlight in the back of the car. Our feet are hot. Our eyes are sore from sunshine. Heat simmers up from the black tarred lot of Bernie's First and Last Chance.

I said your Mum's malarkey, he comes back singing. She never did give you kids enough vegetables.

*　　*　　*

140

I hide under tables, where I get my information, where I make my own decisions. My mother bends over the body of Miss Anne Cecile Sims whose eyes rise up from her sleep and flutter open, Yes dear, my dear Mrs. Hallissey, she says, and smiles at Mum's kiss on the cheek. Miss Mary Louise Sims raises her hand from its faraway place in the sheets and pats the air in a fragile good-bye, Good-bye, Mrs. Hallissey. It is silent in the residence of Miss Mary Louise Sims and her little sister, Anne Cecile. It is another perfectly tucked-down Saturday and they are losing her again; they are giving her back; Mrs. Hallissey is slipping from them like the thin nightgowns from their shoulders. My mother's laced white shoes ratatat through the parlor as she gives everything a final tug at the end of day, and I am satisfied with what is folded, with what is tucked away.

Hey Sweetheart, she says, and pokes her head like sunset under the table, Let's go home.

Where you go, already I am.

Muriel's Dad

✎ Blackberries and cherries sit lightly and ripe in ✎ our hair, bounced from their branches when we scramble and itch. Cross-legged on the garage roof we play in a tangle of treetops and overgrown bushes, looking strange and expensive in the heat of summer, all wrapped up in three yards of red velvet, twirling around inside it, being the monstrous red rose of Muriel and me, till he calls us down. That's three yards a good velvet, her daddy shouts, who means it for the upstairs settee in the furnished apartment.

Here where I learned the first notes of Beethoven's Fifth in Muriel's high house with its sunk-down porches, we bang our vengeance on piano keys, eat spaghetti and sing the multiplication tables until we are ill, charge through the clutter of dusty furniture across the flowered threadbare carpets, hurl ourselves into slapped doors, dig our way to Hell and back in the yard bereft of grass, till he grabs us by the shoulders, one hand each, and tells us we're going for a ride.

Listen you, little Lulie Hallissey, he's saying when he's got me by my shirt, Why don't you just go and dig up your own yard for a change. Bet your mother would have some definite feelings about you digging up the whole neighborhood the way you do. I blink hard when I hear my name, because Mr. Schopenhauer, whom I address with respect in that way, has never once called me by my name in all the years he's known me. Muriel trails behind us on our way to the car in the damp narrow path between houses where the sun never shows its face. He lets go of my shirt and it's a mystery to me but his hand stays lightly on my shoulder. I have to tuck in my chin and look, just to make sure it's still there; looks so much like puff pastry, just about its color and weight, it makes me hungry.

Muriel sits in the front car seat with her daddy. We take the highway downtown. He's got to show us the view of Pittsburgh mills again, once the horizon of his day-shifts, now visited, mourned along the train tracks. At the 12 o'clock whistle, he pats her knee, consoling himself at the loss of lunch in the company of men. Muriel kicks her feet when he touches her, and with the back of her hand tosses her blond hair at me who sits, a witness to their way of life, smack in the middle in the back. Her daddy's neck is sore with summer, bumped with tiny pinks along the collar of his white shirt. Poor Mr. Schopenhauer. He's so nice.

Now he puts his head to the wheel, reaches under

the seat where he has the darkness memorized. Muriel's very own daddy, Mr. Martin Schopenhauer, keeps about every known nutty thing in this world under his front car seat, in the glove box, or tossed in the back, all his prized possessions. He reads "Hints from Heloise" every day of his life and knows what to save and knows by heart all fifty-four ways of warding off tornadoes with paper clips, of which he has thousands, absolutely thousands, every bent down, rusted and screwed up paper clip, he's got. There he is, hammering away at one in his cellar like a poor old soul. Then he'll put some of Mrs. Schopenhauer's metal wax on it and there it is, some lousy paper clip, all reborn, and he stands there, sure as Jesus. It makes you want to stamp your feet or cry, it's so important. Then he tries to give them to you and nobody ever wants them, more than just a little.

His hand pads along the floor under the seat and comes out clung with tobacco and a paper bag. He snaps the bag like a magic man, floop, but it opens sadly, used three times by Mrs. Schopenhauer and then she gives it to him. He sits in Mrs. Schopenhauer's living room for about an hour every month refolding paper bags, putting five gumbands around each stack. When a gumband breaks, he ties it together again and again until it looks like something you could torture somebody with. And the same goes for all his bits of rope, which he gets out now from the glove box. Stay pretty, he says to Muriel. I roll down the window and watch.

Now he stoops by the railroad tracks and his ankles show. He's collecting bottle glass for Muriel again, gathering up the lost. She keeps all the pieces in old mayon-

naise jars, some of which are clunking around my feet in
the back seat, attracting gnats. She lines them up on the
living room sill, a row of seven so far, all identical, shades
of green and bits of darkness from beer bottles, and for
some reason beyond me, she's allowed to trash up the
whole neighborhood this way, except for one moment, if
you should pass by the house, you can see the sun die
down into bits of color, in the Ann Page Mayonnaise jars.
So that's paper bags.

The rope, he uses to tie up old loose pipes he finds
by tracks or for old loose tracks he finds by the pipes. It
really doesn't matter to him, so long as he finds something
that will make him a hero, and it will because he builds
contraptions. Everybody needs a contraption now and
then, especially Mr. Schopenhauer. So that's rope. He ties
all his bits of used life to the roof of the Rambler wagon.
We cast a shadow of some strange animal, mammoth and
extinct. Muriel bounces with excitement; he imagines
everlasting mansions covered in self-stick vinyl; I keep
my trap shut and we get home, hauling their antiques. So
okay, you love what you can.

Unload, he tells us. But Muriel's lost interest. Oh
Daddy, she says. And we climb down to suffer in his
cellar with a sack of potatoes, roasting them in the old
box stove, while we tell our stories of men on the devil's
horses. Eyes dancing on the fires of Hell, we think on it,
think on those fires of Hell, fire everlasting kept on our
arms. Beyond all mercy forever, we charge into the poor
kingdom of his yard, where we set small fires at our own
feet and break his heart, his hope for grass.

Mr. Schopenhauer has handed over his garage to our

145

dream of a mansion in the alley. Behind his back, we have painted the window glass blue, and weekly against his wishes, we haul the good old rickety antiques he gave us into the yard, hose down the floor, make mud, and pray it'll dry before he spits tobacco at us like he does the flies. We rearrange the furniture and set up house all over again, unaware of how hopeless it is, on a muddy floor. Here in his yard, yearly we put on a circus, practice for weeks, and he is the only one, besides my brother Eddy, who ever comes and pays a nickel. If I'm not with Eddy, this is where I am, endless and seasick in Mr. Schopenhauer's yard. We yaw and pitch on swings he made of pipes and chains; we slam and twist on bumpy ice rinks we make every December, hosing down the yard, with Bing Crosby crooning on the hi-fi from the window; and every summer we try one foot in his homemade wading pool eerie with moss and mud, our toes scraped sore by the work of his impatient trowel; and with his rusty golf clubs for canes and the wind for a hat, we tap dance and sing "Swannee River" on our knees; we bang on the smashed lids of his garbage cans; we languish in a prison behind a silver gate he cannot fix that scrapes a rusted hollow in his sidewalk from the years of us, until we are twelve and finished with it forever.

I sit on Mrs. Schopenhauer's sofa. He undresses for dinner in the living room with one eye fixed on the *Six O'Clock Wrestling*, which Mrs. Schopenhauer never misses. His white shirt, still inhabited by the part of him that wore it yesterday and the day before, ribboned with wrinkles and the frowns of the damned, is gray. Mr. Schopenhauer is not perfect. Singing through his teeth,

146

striding across the floor to his own music, he walks around the house in his undershirt, ready for dinner. His chin is blue as mud.

We eat hotdogs with mayonnaise from silver pie tins in the blue light of the wrestling match: Muriel, Mrs. Schopenhauer, Mr. Schopenhauer (Marty, I think to myself), and me. Little bird, he tells me, You eat like a little bird. Then he grunts and slaps his knees after a rush of hotdogs, We're done; though I am only starting.

He strides, on tiptoes, a large ballerina, across the floor in front of Mrs. Schopenhauer's console TV to the baby grand where his shirt hangs from the open lid. I sit watching from the sofa as he swings his white shirt through air and onto his back. Confident as a jazzman, his fingers stroll along the buttons, and I bump to the rhythm of it, as he rocks on his toes, tucks in his tails, accomplished in the last blue seconds of the wrestling match. A man grunts and thuds to the hollow floor of the ring. Mr. Schopenhauer whistles through his yellow teeth. He Sunday strolls toward the door, jingling his keys, whistling something sad through a wad of tobacco. I watch the round-shouldered space that he filled in the entrance hall, where from behind the woodwork, he peeks back, gives me a wink, Hey Rat, Wanna come along? because that's what he calls me, Rat, or sometimes Miss, though what's wrong with Lulie or even Louise, I don't know.

Lately they're always going someplace and he can't wait to get out the door. Mr. Schopenhauer has been laid off. He can't make the payments on the piano or Beethoven's body which, he tells us, lies under its lid. Bye Bye Beethoven, he wants us to know. He bites the air

147

when we're in it, or loves us there swimming in the scent of his perfume, something sour and rusty. Wherever he goes the air tastes briefly of old metal, and then he's gone for what seems like good. Suddenly useless and in the mood, he wants to play Car or Root Beer Man with us, be a hero of ice cream. Playing Father, he seems so out of place, a stranger creeping up on us in the high grass, and Muriel jumps, Oh Daddy, when he appears and we get outnumbered. In fits, he busies himself with Dairy Queens, Saturday rides to nowhere, firework displays on muddy hills, quick trips to G. C. Murphy's Five & Dime, where he hurries us down fluorescent aisles, past a flash of colored thread, mechanical toys, a wind-up man who suffers in a bin.

With matching white patent leather pocketbooks, with one crisp hanky inside each and that's it, Muriel and her mum fidget past me, meddling with their gloves, their hips in full swing, goaded on by the car horn. (I am here nearly as often as the furniture. They tend to overlook me.) Through Ann Page Mayonnaise jars, I watch the Rambler squeal out, with Muriel's little gloved hand like a busted balloon getting lost in the distance, in the chips of light. I stay on alone, eating large veined oranges from a silver tin, ducked down into the arms of the dark pink sofa, with my head lolled back, and Listen you, little Lulie Hallissey, I say to myself for no reason while the car disappears.

Waiting on the Corner with the Gray Wind in Our Jacket Sleeves

🖊 With a watery swing to our shoulders, comic book 🖊 heroes, we row through the old neighborhood streets of Shadyside, through the winding backways I never learned, though Eddy knows it all by heart, each alley, apartment-house passage, and lot. I long for home, but Eddy shuffles, needs to mill, hit his heels a bit, and so we do, with a confidence I just make up at seventeen.

This is the last leg of Elwood Street, he says. How can you not know? We lived near here most of life, down the hill at the corner of Dorothy and Elwood, he tells me. You're in the clouds, you just don't see things, you were always like that.

I flutter him off with my hand, and his eyes blink, a soundless, bewildered artillery. Maybe I'm just seriously unattached, I shrug at Eddy, who comes and goes as he likes now that he has a Pontiac, and I hardly ever see him anymore.

But on this tired day, in a fit of inspiration, lying still on the slant of a hill in Mellon Park, we made it through ten innings together; without moving a muscle, we crowded the empty field with dream batters, like who we used to be.

In the fried dust of the playing field it was always me and them, the licorice-scented boys, about to divvy up. It was always Eddy, the captain, on five toes, and then he landed, surefooted, surprise ballet, and with a swing he'd kick the red dusty ground. With a breath of dust swirled up around his knees, he'd spit and get first pick.

The serious blue kites of his eyes would dart over us then and wobble near my whipped back hair. Snapping his head like a crackerjack in my direction, I'll take *her*, he'd say. Woo woo, what's the hell with you, she's a girl. That's no girl, he'd swear it with a vengeance to the rambling boys, that's my sister.

His arm outstretched, I'd shimmy in. Near where his heart did ballet in his chest. His hair, stiff with sweat, poking out in a jagged circle along the hard cardboard rim of his black and gold baseball hat. Like counted blades of grass, as many as forgiveness. I always knew how many.

No matter what, Eddy always thought I was good enough, though I knew for sure I wasn't. And so I tumbled, I wrangled, I wrestled with rooftops, shinnied like I knew it. I'd shoot around the block, I was always running, I leapt over anything. But every step I took got memorized in my watery head. I would know the way down, the way out, the way back from where he led me, to rooftop, coal mine, hoods of trucks, and I would do it all again, climb, shinny, wrangle, and slide—exact, the way I did it one perfect time before.

That's it, you got it, Lu, wait'll I show them, he'd say with a shiver in his head, just like he invented me, like he drew me on the wind, what an artist, first prize, in air.

Follow me! he'd say, and my body hung midair with a smile on its face. Because of Eddy my fingers bit every hollowed-out gutter along the edge of every black tarred roof on Walnut Street. While he climbed loose and free of the ground I could never stop hoping for, I'd dangle from the roof's thin edge, sprouted from my hands. Every part of me was living, even my dead elbow bones tingled. My body was a trained fire blazing between two buildings. With no mother, no father, no memory, no other ability than to be what sprang from me in all directions like beams of light: to be fingers, chin, and hands, to be forearms flat in guttered leaves, to be that one stretched leg, one last effort, and it was over in the black soup of a rain-watered roof. I sat there in my body. I sat there, found, cross-legged by his side, accomplished in the black soup of the roof.

Or we'd go fishing. In a pond like two famous people. With Grandpap's scissors, two wobbly sticks, and the shimmer of string. I'd catch some screamy black fish with legs all ancient, and yell my head off till he rid it with a giggle, That's a crab. Then's the time for worms again, old eelys. And O little sister, he'd say, You've got to learn to put on worms yourself. Then he'd get this serious look on his face (which is what Eddy got famous for, gave us that look like an oldie, like a teary sweet song the way he always did it, croon croon). He'd elbow me out of earshot of his friends, where he'd put his arm around me, say: You know I ain't going to be with you all your life to put on worms forever; how many times have I got to tell you, here's what happens someday, see, we're two people, about six feet of us each, so Ah hell he'd say and his eyes would think, Let's not worry about it now. Then hooked the worms himself, thank God. So how's fishin'? someone would ask. He'd jerk his head like a spit in my direction, And she puts on worms herself, he'd say. So that's winking and for the while, bound in glory like a double. So who's yourself? Who's you? asked the picture on the water. And shizam, with one answer, there we were. With a slip of the wind, our faces collided.

Or at 6 A.M. in the foggy streets, abandoned but for the two of us and badmen, we delivered Eddy's newspapers at dawn, with a gentle aim at doorways, in the turns of pale green hallways, thud thud thud, the Pittsburgh *Post-Gazette*, dead center down the line, ten points even. Side by side we trailed through the streets of Shadyside and with a crack of our hands folded and tucked the papers, neat and trim. But in the tossing they sometimes came undone, fluttered down to doorsteps, like city pigeons making a big show of their wings. We didn't care, except we'd fix them anyway and drift back home in the state of grace, confessing the love of some new girl, comparing our heroes of baseball to the death. We trailed home single-file through dimlit streets, closing our eyes in the last familiar stretch of Dorothy Avenue, telling the swirls of the city we saw inside, chips of light leftover from the vision of each other's clothes, until, with a gentle smack of sunrise by the time we reached the porch, something brief like the day was born just above our heads.

So what the heck, he said one Saturday afternoon, climbing with his baseball bat to the high hoods of trucks left to languish and rust in the lot behind our father's house, Let's do something that hurts. My eyes watched through the fingers of my hands where light was pink, as his bat swung into glass, making webs and fountains, sprays of glass. I climbed up and made one fraidy whack, which is when Dad came sliding sideways down the hill, pretending to be our father. What the heller you kids doing? I'm calling the cops on you damn kids.

Risking arrest, we ran through a small handful of woods. I narrowed down after Eddy into the ground, into the jaw of the earth, to the abandoned coal mine behind our father's house. Inside the cramped black we screamed. Our voices shivered down the coal from the walls into our hair. When he whacked his bat into earth's old side, a crack of black ribs, my mouth sprung open permanent, and I tore upward into him, into the coal webs of his flesh, his ear in my fist. I stood on the back of his neck, punching at the living pinholes of light overhead, my way back up. I landed belly down and reached back in, grabbing for his face gritty with thrown-down earth. With the new tips of his crewcut in my fist, I fished him out, wriggling. So what's your problem? Jumped to his feet, he'd really like to know. And me, gone mad and solitary, arms brilliant, shaking off the tight dark, slapped my complete self into him, aiming at his soul.

You cheater. What a show off. Why you lazy bum. Chief Stick in the Mud. Shut up. Why don't you throw away those socks? Why don't you change your pajamas?

We've been friends now for seventeen years. And just as soon as I got born, there was Eddy, and he's been like a ribbon on my life. Most everywhere he went, he took me too, and I've been like a ribbon on his life.

My brother is strong and thin. There's something in him that's after Heaven but he gets sidetracked. He kisses our mother's hand then stares at his plate, begging forgiveness again for stolen tires, ten hot bags of licorice stashed under his bed, another lie. Pale and smooth, then suddenly athletic, he moves with the flick of a ribbon. If he had his choice, he'd rather not hurt you or yell back across the table at the end of summer, he'd rather imagine the long winters when he no longer sees so much of you; how unfamiliar you will become.

But today I am alive to him and my brother is alive and I mean that as the highest compliment. Today he made me like him completely. He cried on the slant of a hill in Mellon Park. Whenever he cries (and he will if you tell him a story of when you were children, as if you'd just given him everything he always wanted when you remember the color of his pea-green coat; the debacle of Grandpap's scissors—rusted like that, it's a shame, says Mother, you kids always putting things into water for no reason; or what he saved his money for on your thirteenth

birthday, a jade ring now lost between two neighborhoods; what he said; where he went; how his eyes look
just like Mummy's; and then he'll talk for hours and his
memory is a genius), it's to me, the sister. I am his
witness. I swear never to tell. I speed down the highways,
hitting eighty-five, and grant all of his wishes. He cries
and grants all of mine. Some part of us still lives in a
world that had us in it as children, when we lowered our
empty shoes, one each, by laces into Highland Pond, for
no explainable reason except to know: two lost shoes
forever at the bottom of a pond.

He loans me his car, and I listen to the reasons why
he cries. With the softness of poured milk he cries, Fed
up to here, he says, when he cares too much, and he
cannot stand to love like that. He cares for our father. I
narrow my eyes. He waits for him as he always waited, on
his own, for hours on the front porch steps, with an
impossible faith possible to him only, singing Daddy's
Sinatra songs to himself. He's always been the only one
who won't give up. When Dad's had too much to drink, we
know where to find him, curled up in the back seat of my
brother's Pontiac LeMans, his very first brand-new ap-
pliance. I hate appliances, cars, toasters, hi-fis, and all I
own, I want it to be in a pack on my back, while he says
Ah Jeez, and goes out to buy a stereo.

Daylight, moonlight, and all the passing trains. We
sit some evenings on somebody's stoop. A parade of boys
bobs up the street and side to side, church-solemn about
being boy. Hiking up their spirits, they shiver, Hey.
Putting on the ritz of meanness, a splash of glory, they

spit at our feet. So come on, old man. His public school people pass by. He joins in and slaps an ass. So see you. So don't be late for supper.

And lately I get furious at some people for no reason, just because they smell like toast or wear this ratty old robe at breakfast or make these certain noises with their teeth, which is really not his fault. They haven't been all his own true teeth since he was nine years old, when he nearly died in this roof and tree accident in the rain, climbing high as a dream, swimming through air when I wasn't looking, hitting earth, aiming elsewhere.

Propelled by the fins of trouble, that boy always was banging into something. He has always been my official responsibility. Watch out for Eddy, Keep an eye on Eddy, my mother always told me that. I memorized him, every sweet devil move of his bones that went ahead anyway with what I couldn't stop. Mother, when she heard the news that Eddy was taken to the hospital, and I told her, threw her umbrella up in the air. And still to this day, we say a Rosary for that boy, sometimes a whole nine-day novena behind his back. Our mother's umbrella snagged on the pines, then floated down like sorrow. He lived, felt chosen, he said, but for what? he asked; our mother's umbrella rolled free across the grass, and he became a man.

So here we are in Mellon Park on this tired day, survived, on our elbows, like some big deal, after all these years. The sun makes a tinsel of everything that's got an edge and gets you blind. He tugs down on the brim of his baseball hat, the way he's done for years, trying to make the scar on his forehead not show, but it always does, I can always see it.

I hate everything lit up. Everything's got a meanness, and a poverty, too. Some lousy patch of brown on the Nabisco Cracker Factory that stretches a whole block along the side of the park on Penn Avenue. And on the grass, all the dead Dairy Queen cups. Why they always litter where you come from? This world, we say, drifting in and out of imaginary innings and cities in our minds. And in a hush we talk of the riots in Newark and Detroit, while the factory is busy with the holy work of crackers, stacks blowing out their smoke into the sky's pale wafer; it tips on our tongues, our heads thrown back into the smell of cookies.

So here we are, pretending home in a puff of old Shadyside grass. Just moved to East Liberty, to a view of Sears, Roebuck and Cool Care All Kind Refrigeration Company, with prefab city houses and Lehmann's Department Store up the block. Mother nearly lives at Lehmann's, now that she's been promoted to manager of Lamps. We all miss the old neighborhood, what it used to be. Somebody rich bought our old house on Dorothy Avenue. They tore off the front porch, like tearing off the lap of a beautiful woman.

I hate modern architecture. Everything's built to stare back at you like a U.S. Marine, pop-eyed with terrific posture. It's hard to find anything round or womanly in buildings anymore. Then yesterday, all these goons covered Sears with turquoise siding, and I hate bright things.

The sun beams down over Mellon park. In the mid-

157

dle of an easy out, one of my best men gets blinded by the sun and brother-life gives me his cap. Brother-shade has enough love, could be an oak tree, and me such a fuss. It's imagination, Lu, he tells me. Nothing has to go wrong.

Apologizing now, I hit my heels on the curb and do what he likes. But thank God the sun sinks down in the middle of a dare. In a bone chill I know more than anything, in me permanent, I'm always cold, I quiver. The gray wind roams, an old animal in my jacket sleeves. Hey, brother, says the famous sister-whine, Let's get the hell back home. I get the lonelies in this light, have to make my getaway toward something eternal like supper, the smell of roasted meat.

Twilight topples down over us from rooftops like gutter rain, and the half hour is a sad holiday or a mongrel I'm pretending to love for a little while longer, while he truly does: all the space, the space. So Eddy, me, and twilight mill like we could maybe get away with murder. Daylight like a jailbreak is over. We hang around like a legend of blasted-out coops to nowhere. Night gives me the willies. Crickets begin it with their high-pitched wings. Locusts swell. He finds a body, silvery black. I shut my eyes against its dried-out shell, a dead thing, he dangles it, and chases me home. Wound up in tight circles on the fire escape, sister-whine says, You jackass, I quit, I'm telling on you, I swear I'll tell. Then we come in laughing, me so fussy about dead things.

Eddy sets the Melmac plates down delicate as time bombs, while I sing spoon, any word five times, to a melody of our bumped selves (including Helen at the last

158

possible minute, she's always late, on her way out the door, changing her clothes the color of saltwater taffy, or talking on the telephone for hours to anyone who isn't us), in a tango of shared labor, back and forth, across the yellow kitchen until Mother scatters in, breathing hard. Like a private eye with fancy eyes shifting under the invisible brim of my hat, I count the food on everybody's plate, prongs of broccoli, tomato slices, measure in my mind the diameter of pork chops, making sure every last one of us around here gets treated equal, fair and square, except for Grandpap, he can have whatever he likes, while the night swoops down outside, makes off with the small body of the day in its starry beak. Nobody, including me, gets cheated when I'm in charge.

And as for dessert, I tuck my portion of plums or cake in the far back of the refrigerator. I save my portion, I won't use it up ever, but I will think on it, my share of whatever it is. I will save it until it is melted, until it is blue with mold, and I will toss it, feeling bereft, except for the fact that I had it for days, I had it slowly, for weeks in my mind, my share of whatever it was.

After every last evidence of our late supper is swept away, I slip through the loophole of the family, which is always allowed. Be who you want to be, my mother always says, Do what you have to, you know what's right.

In the bright yellow bedroom I share with my sister, I take out a real wood cedar chest, made by Lane as a miniature model, which my father once gave to my mother as a promise for a larger one, as I now promise myself a larger life than what is preserved here in a hieroglyphics of ticket stubs, dandelion stems, gum

159

wrappers, all this trash I used to feel so sentimental and teenage about. I feel relieved when things mean nothing to me anymore for the rest of my life, like signatures at the edges of valentines, except for Joseph McMead's on a card with a donkey dressed as a mailman, that springs out from the center with a paper kiss, the very first I ever received.

Think fast, snaps Eddy, tumbling into my room, tossing an apple, a rare baseball, anything he's got. Son of a gun, I say, Stop it. He dives from the house, skinny as a crack of doorlight, into the future, into all that space, and I go back to my papers, dumping them in the trash. Once a year from now on, I sit cross-legged on the floor and throw things out of my brain and my closets. I figure if anyone would ever want to investigate me for some reason, there's going to be very little evidence to go on.

When we moved from Dorothy Avenue we left behind the furniture that was given to us secondhand, what we grew up with, pretending it was new, pretending so well that we were proud of it, until we saw it on the curb by the van. Leave it, said Mum. I called Goodwill like I really meant it. We gave away all my old toys a second before I didn't need them anymore, but beat-up dolls I kept, and seeing them now, with their eyes rolled back, in a one-armed, one-legged heap in the dark of the closet, I remember how I strung them by their fingers or toes from doorknobs, and poor dollies, poor little boys and girls, I think to myself, as if they were a race of people. So let's just say I hugged the pillars of the house on Dorothy Avenue one last time, ran back inside to hear the furnace kick off, echoing in stripped rooms, and say light streaming through the windows taught me one last time and I left.

Mainly I have a stack of drawings, these saved by my mother who saves everything we created as gifts to her with a lot of love work in them, really dippy stuff, aerial views of monstrous sinks and refrigerators. People used to come around and ask just what it was I was drawing, especially nuns, What's that? But I was just pleasing myself with a color that was there, or with the shape of a line like a twirl. And the twirl was nothing but pleasure, though it soon became chimney smoke, a cloud, curly-headed grass or girl. Nothing ever really gets lost inside you. The slightest thing could be of use someday.

At an early age, heart-shaped birds rained down from the sky and into the kitchen. Then I grew older. I drew the world as if it were reasonable or real. Branches were branches and arms were arms. Then something worse happened. I colored inside the lines like somebody just too good and right all the time, which my sister says I am, like the right hand of God on earth, judging all Pittsburgh if I could, always with oughta this and that. So alright. Some kids used to say, So the windows are on the floor, the stars are in the grass, the sheriff gets arrested. So who cares? So okay. I did.

My family of sticks is perfectly wooden. The rhinoceros no longer sits down to dinner. Under a leaping of musical notes, a little boy shows his muscle to the clapping mummy, the happy father smokes his pipe, gets his slippers from a dog, and dances with the mum, while the girls hold on, a row of easy targets with banana smiles, with their arms outstretched, the ground a tightrope, the

161

windows of the house behind them heavily draped, row upon row of shut eyes.

Then there's this big congregation of diaries I've kept, mainly a lot of ha ha this and ha ha that. I'd rather draw than write or walk or talk or anything, mainly because there's nothing to say. Even if there is someday, I'd rather not be the one who says it, unless it's a sin if I don't.

About to enter my last year of high school, where, if they had asked me in the first place, I would have told them I didn't want to go, I sit on the fire escape and read the distant signs:

Al & Sidney's AC DC New & Used Cool Care Co.
Experts in Walk-In Reach-In Boxes
Compressor Replacements Sold over the Counter

The Nylon Bridal Illusion Company
Rent or Buy Your Maid-de-France
Tulles, Veils and Accessories, Rhinestone Crowns
Maline Veilings, Excellently Dyed

McNulty's Religious and Botanical Products Company
Specializing in Spiritual Books & Curios
Relics, Perfumes, & Oils

Late evenings in half-light, I spend mainly in the yard, alone and pole vaulting with my mother's aluminum clothes prop, over rope strung tight between two high fences. Our building here in East Liberty used to be called the Astoria Anne until the landlord tore down the black wrought-iron gate from the front and laid this

162

stretch of cement by the garages out back, where a
wrecked Chevy sits abandoned in a nearby yard with the
beams of a house in the back seat, with red roses on a
vine climbing in and out its missing windows.

I pole vault in the half-light. Sometimes my mother
watches from our third-floor window; Eyow! I can hear
her say and pretend I don't. The thin tight stretch of rope
dances in its own glitter, stupidly high, shimmery as a
future. I back off, give my weight to this thin pole, then
purely to nothing, to air. Eyes shut, I sail, sure-footed in
the breeze, I'm high, I'm flying low, I'm over over it,
changed and landing in my child body, near to what was
left in other places, abandoned yards.

Nothing will ever come back to me and stay like
Dorothy Avenue. So this is the news they tell me, from the
old neighborhood. House burnt down. We go there now,
each alone, quietly confessing it later, making detours to
visit, one by one, its frail bones, standing in the lot out
back where our games still sing. Nothing will ever be
destroyed like house, where I learned the many names for
things, *barley, Buenos Aires, solar system, psalm*, where I
know it all by heart, by one clear eye.

Dearests

The Family, Afterward

Mrs. Hallissey's Pittsburgh

Anna

⚑ The gray of it was enormous with lamplit houses ⚑ in the late afternoons and fluorescent schools and stores pinned like yellow butterflies against the whitewash of its sky on a rainy day.

At the headwaters of the Ohio, the rivers made it so.

It was more a feeling than a color. It was something Anna knew, as she watched from the windows of the new city bus. It was how she felt, from a far-off place, all things come back into being.

The years made it so. It was the way she remembered the whole downtown; as a child, glancing off her father's gray chin through a trolley-car window, how the great mix of office buildings and warehouse rows, flat-faced or complicated with turrets and arches, resolved itself to the single soaring color of Nicholas Jacob's chin,

or how the wind mixed with the colors of her duntes'
washed-out dresses and colored in the whole city.

The gray of it was as smooth as trolleys on rounded
tracks. And though tracks had vanished from repaved
streets, her mind went on like that, turning corners softly,
her journey muted by a tendency toward a dreamy soli-
tude.

On her way back home from McCabe Funeral Parlor
on the 73 Highland from a cousin's funeral, on her day off
from Lehmann's, the gray of it was white, orange, blue but
changed by rain or smoke or childhood. The smallest of
hillside neighborhoods, where houses hugged the sidewalks awash with dogs and kids, spoke large of its sky;
tiny third-floor windows yellowed with light called up the
sky in contrast and made it vast. She could see it from the
attic rooms of childhood, a gritty orange in 1938, graphite
blowing lightly and black through air from the smoke-
stacks of Jones & Laughlin between Second Avenue and
the Monongahela River. She could see it strung along
riverside highways, swept clear by the long wash and
wrecking ball of the '40s, bridges and rows of grim houses
against the skyline destroyed or hammered to the new,
the whole town blasted clean, or from the new city bus
now, and it was a comfort, recalling parts of God, a tired
and weathered mystery.

How great and simple it seemed with the swing of its
highways onto narrow streets: the city of bridges, dim
taverns, and acres of lawn, the city of steps and red
hillside houses, rows of warm wooden porches, their laps
filled with rain or snow.

I like to count on the same things every day, she

thought. And then the sound of it set in: the squeak of a clothesline, the voices of women calling out weather or advice from the windows, wheels, hammers, the upriver craneman's siren, the 12 o'clock whistle, the 3 o'clock school bells, the 6 o'clock churches, and she liked to imagine the roar of the fallen furnaces, like Jones & Laughlin's Ann or Duquesne's Dorothy Six.

The hammer of it was its holiness, with one hard-working neighborhood to the next, nestled in gray. Its people hauled lunch pails (though did they still do that? she wondered) at 5 A.M., stood on ladders, forged and sheared, they measured, bent, and ladled, sat down to supper, and finally looked up over the curled-down tips of stuffed cabbage. The webwork of their tires and shoes crisscrossed mud puddles in sunlight and dusty lots on the dwindling night shift.

The mills were cutting back and closing plants. That there was furnace, grate, and stove, that there was fire and earth, slab and plate, beams and pilings, that there was still smoke spiraling upward, was glorious, she thought, and the lives of people beneath it, where their hands, their labor made it home.

She knew what home was, it was the tiniest things, a string of labors and consolations. It was peeling something (paring an apple); it was combing something (the fringe on the rug); it was hosing down the sidewalks; it was mulch and bud; the watered trees; what she rescued from a bin. For years now she had been living alone, and she knew how to make a home for herself, how to listen to the sound of Pittsburgh's trains or to rain beating on patched rivers in winters swirled with floes of ice. She knew what to watch for: bridges painted blue or gold but black and glittered with headlights at night; the delicate ironwork of cranes slanted over the waters; stone walls checkered brown and gray; shaded streets with wide sloping lawns; striped Tudors along Highland Avenue, once mansions, now apartments 1 through 3, busy with kitchens, stairwells, and private entrances. She knew what to love: the wiriness of winter trees, branches mixed with telephone wire against a backdrop of clapboard and brick shaded with years of ivy or blasted to the new; white abandoned factories chipped through to brick, with painted windows broken through to blackened warehouse places.

When the 12 o'clock whistle blew, she could see it all, under a corner of its sky. She could see to rivers north and south, to the '40s; and why was it always this: men in the lunchrooms of Pittsburgh, with tomato and baloney sandwiches dangling from their wrists, the sharp folds of Cut-Rite wax paper, lunch spread out on an opened *Sun-Telegraph*, salt and pepper shakers, thick-glassed and squat, with dented tops, their silver lids secured tight by some final never final turn toward serenity. The thought of the shakers pleased her. Salt and pepper years ago, splashing down neatly over garden tomatoes.

She loved the little details of people's lives, what they had for lunch that day, the colors of their clothes, while the city stood in backdrop and let it all unfold. How the old ones stepped, what the girls of East Liberty Lehmann's had for dinner (she stopped to talk early morning in the parking lot), how their babies were born and their fathers died; or when, on one of the very rare times she went to a restaurant for dinner, the most amazing things happened: she saw the lady full in the face, singing in her meat-stained apron. Imagine that (and it weighed on her just a little), how the kitchen help came out like that to sing "Happy Birthday" at your table.

Now that was something she would have liked to tell her father. On the day he died (it was years ago), he kept asking for his scissors, and ever since she wondered why, and the question of the tailor's scissors mixed with everything, with bus rides, happy birthdays, and funerals. The scissors occurred to her at the oddest times. I have to cut this, he kept saying. She wondered if he had been making a beautiful coat in his mind.

She missed her dad. She would have liked to tell him about her birthday, ask him about the scissors, or about her one regret: What was my mother like? She wished she had known more about her mother. But she would tell her girls at work. She would go in to work tomorrow and tell Mary Malinic about the woman in the meat-stained apron singing "Happy Birthday."

Women, she thought, they were such a relief. She enjoyed their company. Not that she wanted to get too close, but she liked to help them along. She had so many daughters now; they came to her like birds. She touched their shoulders; their backs were sore and she touched them because Hey, she thought, she needed to touch someone gently, every once in a while; and they sighed, What a relief. The men made fun when they found them in the stockroom on their break, drinking coffee she brought in a thermos, eating rolls she bought from the bakery, with cloth napkins she brought from home.

171

She had waited for the 73 Highland for an hour and a half. Just like a man, she had said to herself, there's one every ten minutes. Then suddenly it occurred to her, standing there at the bus stop: blue dogs that played "Stardust." Funny, but the smallest things were coming back to her lately. It was a sudden revelation. She'd get home and tell her visiting daughter. Louise was always asking questions, scribbling down the answers, and here she had one, she had an answer: blue dogs that played "Stardust." There were these little blue china dogs your daddy loved. She would tell her a story. Your sister's closet, she'd say. Your daddy made it from vegetable crates, where we hung calico curtains and placed on top, blue dogs that played "Stardust."

She was slipping back, she was going forward. They would discuss Louise's future (Did she love New York and why? And next time make sure, bring Franny too— funny, but she didn't know when it began, her waiting for Franny to come home with Louise for a good long visit). They would discuss what a lovely woman, that Franny, and they would discuss the recent flood down South. What with all this rain it was on her mind. Those poor people, she'd tell her. Whenever I think of a river, I think of home and I see something I love very much going down the river, like my pictures, Picasso's *Blue Boy* in the hall, Fragonard's *Young Girl Reading* over my bed, my jewelry box, my telephone. If we have a flood, dig up my crocuses first thing. They're too nice and fat to leave.

And my poetry books, she'd tell her. She'd climb to the high back of the closet and hand them down. Poetry, she'd tell her, You know I used to love poetry. And she would show her daughter all the unexpected places marked by violets that had become the impression of violets—Tennyson, Whittier, Dickenson, Elizabeth Barrett Browning—and tell her, Look how nice they lay upon my bed.

On her way back home from McCabe Funeral Parlor on the 73 Highland, the houses, their clumps of brick, sat satisfied under their roofs, and the parked unworried humps of cars in front gave her peace. She stopped off at the Variety Store on Walnut Street for buttons and cards, and at the Grand View Florist Shop, where she was determined on hands and knees, searching through cardboard vases, to find two good strands of pussy willow. It was too expensive. Out of season, it looked so disappointing. But she was so willing for it to be gorgeous. Kneeling at the toes of the haughty florist, she would take her time, she would choose her own.

She liked buying gifts. She liked sending hankies in cards to anyone who did her the slightest favor. For the first time in her life she had the money; her kids were grown; they had their own apartments, their own suburbs and cities. She had a spare room now where she installed twenty-two feet of metal shelving to fill with all sorts of little things: cuckoo clocks, pots and pans, towels and blankets, intended as gifts for her children or near strangers: unwed teenage mothers, women recently divorced with ten children, the one lady cab driver in this whole world who's attending night school, and who lives with this other nice lady who's a bartender studying to be a nurse. It seemed like everyone she met lately was on their way to some better place in life and working hard to do it. She would help them along.

God knows, so many people along the way had helped her to where she was: the manager of three departments on the top floor, Lamps & China, Towels & Linens, Draperies & Rugs, at the East Liberty Lehmann's. She felt a great allegiance to her store. Lehmann's had made their life possible. Though funny, she thought, whenever she dreamt of it and she dreamt of it often, she was always in the basement; I have never been to the third floor in my dreams, she realized; I'm always in the basement, wandering through rows of small appliances and racks of bicycles.

She was always working overtime in her dreams. I'm gonna die with my boots on, she always said that. My kids are going to be rich, she decided. My only regret is no husband to give some money to. You know you're better off when you die and have a husband. If only he could have lived long enough, she thought, if only I could have fed him, though she was no one's widow, she had left nearly thirty years ago, and she had her own name. She had it on paper now. Anna Evaline Jacob. Even though everyone still called her Mrs. Hallissey.

People knew her all along Penn Circle: You're that nice little lady from Lehmann's, Mrs. Hallissey, the one who wears all the hats and has three little kids; and she'd laugh, Not so little and I'm not Mrs. Hallissey anymore. Except maybe in some far-off place, she thought; Mrs. Hallissey was the squeak of a hinge, a door left slightly ajar in a small house miles ago, though that's what they called her all these years, even though it wasn't so, Mrs. Hallissey from Lamps & China.

From the bus window, life was in a rush with newly peaked roofs, bulldozers and construction workers, vanished cousins and husbands (it was years ago) who died too young, fathers calling out for scissors, florist shops and fountains, circular roadways and a pedestrian mall. Set on their legs, things tottered and turned about, or deep-rooted and good as rock, they held on and insisted. Laundry lines confessing their clothes, church pews, parking lots, Regent movie seats, the maroon velvet baring its teeth, boxcars with no engines. All that stuff on the minds of angels, she thought, the slightest things: cabbage, school uniforms, old Forbes Field, though it was a little blasphemous, some would say, to think like that.

East Liberty Presbyterian, on the corner of Penn and Highland, had its doors swung open. When she used to attend Mass, she was never one to sit in the back of a church. Up front was the place to be, where sunlight snagged on the sparkled pieces inside stone pillars and was easily confused with fish scale, wing of insect, something blessed, iridescent. Across the years, she had so many dreams of churches, of being lost in church, of wandering far off into its cellar or bell tower, of losing her shoe. In the dreams, her children were always little; she needed help; she had lost her shoe. When the nice man from the third row went to retrieve it for her from one of the tiny balconies, he fell and died. The shoe was yellow, lost and found, and she was mortified, all that sorrow from a little yellow shoe. It had lasted so long.

But she was no hell-and-holy-water kind of Catholic

175

now. I don't belong, only on my own terms, she said. Some people think I have too much to say, but hey, that's what the gospels were all about. The girls quote me; word gets around and a few of us change.

A window on the move, dotted with rain, where the city appeared speckled and eerie with river fog, was more answer than she could have prayed for, and she was determined to have something to say to Louise. She would tell her the dream of the yellow shoe; she would keep a list of dreams, of this and that, on the backs of grocery lists, and tuck them in her bureau drawer, for sooner or later; she would mention Guy Hallissey's love (of the blue china dogs), the rain, the church, the over-due bus.

She was slipping back, she was going forward, gathering up the full extent of the day, her arms wrapped tight around brown paper bags, a hodgepodge of flowers and buttons. Off in the distance, a hazy factory stack blended with its sky; a cousin's soul mixed with smoke, arose; and the dead of Pittsburgh, all the living and to come, buttoned down against the cold, or opened their collars to its wind, as she did, stepping from the bus onto the sidewalk, where the light rain was a comfort, the washed-down streets, and the thought of the living tucked safely in rented rooms.

Our Father's Room

Helen and Louise

⏧ Except for the white enameled coffee pot spotted ⏧ with grime, important on the single-burner hot plate, except for the coat hangers balanced on a nail by the door, the room where our father lived during the last years of his life, where we went just once on a day in summer of 1968, gave the impression of home, but home tucked into home, stripped down, made miniature; faded, so it left the impression of black and white.

A chenille spread, a relic of pink, whitened and thin, pulled tight across the bed, and tucked vaguely under pillows, felt soft like summer grass where we sat; but it was a winter of a room. It was a shadow of a room breached by two windows, interrupted by daylight, a room still and poised in the months before he died at the age of forty-eight.

The room lacked gravity, stripped of the million unnecessary familiars, the immortal gadgets and burdens of home. What little there was inside seemed to hover in its place, detached and solitary, as if the furniture had arrived by accident, by no one's particular intention. Because of architecture or a frame of mind, the farthest small corners of it under the eaves were left unlit; half of the room where he lived seemed to have slipped his attention, undiscovered, or simply left behind, unfurnished and forgotten.

We don't remember what street we were on, what lay on either side of us, or below, the curious hallways of his coming home, the unknown rooms with boarders by the week, unremembered or never seen, or seen only in the shadows of a late afternoon half-promising rain.

Although it was a third-floor room of slanted ceilings, with its peaked roof intersecting the telephone wires, it felt low and burrowed from the earth, as if our father, like something ancient and tired, softened by fatigue or a new sweetness, was tunneling through his days.

We sat on the bed with our father. His knee is resting there and is still very clear to us, though we may have invented it as something sure to keep (the bend of one leg in brown trousers against the chenille bedspread). Yes, his knee is resting there, and our brother casts his willowy shadow over it from where he stands beside him, curved and solicitous and careful as a ribbon, pleased at this new sight of us together. We are midair, detached of neighborhood, affiliation. We are third floor, a good climb up, and here as if by happenstance, father and daughters and son.

Our father is the gift our brother has brought us to by the hand, down a hallway we can't remember, in a part of Pittsburgh we can't recall. Eddy is pleased with himself for having done this. We are a reunion, a fountain that springs from his clear boy heart. He is nineteen years old. We are twenty-two and eighteen.

That we're clear about. Not the rightness of the numbers at their place in time, we may be guessing, not the rightness of our bodies that stood or sat beside him where they once had or not, but the rescue of a few minutes, a settling down sometime before he died.

We sat with our father. It occurred to us to look at him from the very tops of our eyes, over the frames of our glasses that established the horizon we kept ourselves beneath, tucked away from him. And as we sat there we felt ourselves drifting backward, light of weight, like blown leaves, into the unlit corners.

Whenever our father entered a room, it was with an easy, too-quick stride, with a grin too large, the hello too loud. With arms just at the start of opening, he strode forward, his body loose with a joy we found incomprehensible and false. So give your daddy a hug, he'd say. But he was too much, as a stallion would be too much, galloping toward us in an open field. But more, his stride lacked the truth of the stallion with its muscle, each tendon unloosed of any sadness. This father striding toward us was no pure galloping expression of joy but something concocted. We would back against the farthest point of the room, the backs of our knees bumping against the radiator, a refrigerator, a chair, the wall. We would each look at him that way then, from the tops of the eyes, not knowing

179

what knowledge we were putting together. And now we sat on the bed with our father, still vaguely discomforted, but appeased by his quiet, our heads lowered over a handful of his tie pins that he has spilled from a small wooden box into the palms of our hands.

The cascade of tie pins into our hands, the tinkling sound of it, its streaming of silver and gold, reminds us now of water, a thin clear creek in sunlight along Nadine Road, a blacktop off Allegheny River Boulevard, where our father would take his three children on younger Saturdays to wash one of his many boatlike cars across the years, cars that were always impossibly large like billboards or the sides of houses, colored turquoise or yellow like sticks of butter. The clear ancient smell of the creek, of its good earth and tree roots, clung to the wash rags and our short damp clothes. And in the intensity of our efforts, our skin and hair were creek water, and there was blue enough from the sky to notice the crisp cracker white of his rolled cuffs, enough green woods to notice the flowerlike flashes of our colored shirts and shorts, enough plain Saturday to love without thinking, darting between car and creek with good healthy ragfuls of water. In these moments of scrubbing down to a sparkle the turquoise immensity of the muscled Chevy or the fin-tailed grace of the Pontiac convertible, our father and his three children reached a rare unblinking silence in the peace of a wooded road, unvisited except for what belonged most intimately: sunlight, father, daughters, earth, creek, and son.

It is incongruous to think of our father in sunlight, but he is there, given to the earth and its wind. There is

always one sideways glance, unimportant and plain, leftover, like a crumb or a morsel, and from this small thing
(the sight of him standing midturn by the left headlight of
the Pontiac, with the wind at his trousers, sunlight flood-
ing his white shirt, with a coveted yellow sponge cupped
in both hands) comes a vision invented entire, comes an
entire lifetime we might conjure up in a flying second.

Imagine him then at 6 o'clock each day. From the
tops of our eyes, that snatch of a father could become a
life he once lived, filled in with thoughts of supper and a
change of clothes, with somewhere to be by 7. We sat in
our father's room and there was nothing but the clear
sailing of our eighteenth and twenty-second years, their
narrow unbothered sweep suddenly bothered by love for
our father, a strange tugged-at reluctance.

Imagine him then. He is coming home each evening
from a good job on the daylight shift, tossing his keys into
the darkness of a bureau top. But the keys go whirling far
out into space, light miles away, along the spine of the
universe. Trying to remember our father now, it is like
that, as if we too had tossed something out into the air (a
key, a penny, a paper, the word *daddy*) with the intention
of sure safe landing on a known land, but it has been
whirling all these years.

We knew little. We asked after him now and then.
But there was really no question for which we wanted an
answer. The porthole through which we occasionally
glanced at his life was window enough. Our father moved
on his own path, no longer at top speed, midleap, jumping
through the hoops of his own high hopes, but earthbound,
dogged, even gentle, weighed down by mementos feather

light, a small box of tie pins, a drawerful of dotted handkerchiefs, curled photographs of a Siberian husky, and a
'49 Plymouth with rolled upholstery, with a fierce gri-
mace nosing out from its silver grill.

And, what surprised us, there were photographs of
his children with bobbed hair or crewcut, of Mother as if
she still existed as a wife, and of the swing set on Franklin Way as if it were not rusted and long gone, but still
functioning as the hand-built squeaky centerpiece of
childhood.

He was dredging things up. From his back pocket, a
tiny case of black and white photographs. He had
trimmed the photographs small and unevenly to fit the
plastic pages where his children still played in daylight.
They hung back or burst forward, they rubbed their eyes
and frowned or smiled, held still or danced, and somehow
grew like weeds, freely, unassuming, bounding out of
their shoe sizes, bursting from their favorite clothes, but
tugged back somehow by second unanswered thoughts.
They stood their ground with squinted eyes, with shirt-
tails or skirts bunched in their fists. They stood their
ground like wood or stone, or child it seemed, incapable
of argument or witness.

There was always an element of mystery about our
father, not at all compelling, but simply a secret life he
lived apart from us, the further away and deeper set in
silence, the better. It was obvious, we thought, what his
secret life comprised—it was clearly one of alcohol and
of women who called in the middle of night to ask us
where he was. But suddenly, with the small deliberate
case of black and white photographs sprung from his

182

back pocket, we saw that his secret life was his first, it was us, it was home, the plain and level of three children, a wife.

He was dredging us up, dotting a vacated land with signposts and the smallest clues. A bike with six flags, Louise's striped overalls, a bow at the back of Helen's dress, Eddy with so much crewcut he appears bald, a handmade step stool painted green, a yard overrun with dust and tufts of grass, a lopsided fence, his flowered ties and striped jackets, cousins piled on sofas, blue tennis shoes lost from their feet, a nonsense alphabet chalked on the porch boards, misshapen toys. From his back pocket and plastic pages, from a small wooden box, where the years were stored in too-small places, he was dredging things up.

This was speed now. Time was the arrow. It was loss, the speed of gone things. Our father talked excitedly of foreign places we had little or no memory of: Lake Erie, Franklin Way. And as he spoke the years passed by with a lightning grace that almost gave him back his Plymouth, his children, his wife.

I took you kids to Erie, he said, I loved Lake Erie. I took off at the slightest chance. I'd grab you kids and go; we had a big time in summer. I loved summer; I was crazy for June.

There was something he knew. And as he showed us the photographs (two girls on a towel, they were lost, we remembered it, the quiet stretch of sand, That's you, he told us, You thought you were lost but I was right there), we could feel in our father's head a circle's pace of something caged and eager and willing to please, something almost frantic with goodwill, calming itself with the thought of the past.

We sat in our father's room above a wide avenue, and it began to rain, spattering down on third-floor eaves outside the window, into a past, into the half-opened windows of a too-small house in Wilkinsburg where we used to live, a rented house so overheated, he told us, that wallpaper buckled and peeled, and we can picture it now, curled like tiny question marks near the ceiling in the room where the five of us slept, where the kitchen clock, we can imagine, was round and glassed and loud with days, marking them off, where he actually lived (this amazes Louise who can't remember one word, the sound of his footsteps, not a single vision of his face in that house). As far as we both could hear or see, if you could put that together as a sum, the effect was this: he was never really there in any way we could recall clearly, (except for Helen perhaps, who has phrases, words, and maybe stories, perhaps some Christmastime, she'll tell). We looked at him then from the tops of our eyes.

We remember a certain poverty, a cruelty of circumstance we felt was evidenced in the box of tie pins and clasps. A cameo knight, in a gold setting nicked through to tin, seemed like a great secret someone had finally told. A fake turquoise stone, set in curls of silver splintered with fine black lines, seemed like a way of life. He was especially proud of the single glass pearl on its sharp stem. And somehow, we suddenly loved all of them, because of what we knew they finally were.

The held-tight poverty of the tie pins surprised us. His new clothes surprised us as well, his pants bright brown polyester and a matching knit shirt of bold green and white stripes. We could only remember everything worsted and pin-striped, pure cotton or gabardine wool, the silk of fine ribbed socks, matched ties and hankies, bright Florsheim shoes. And years later, the too-large sweaters and rumpled shirts where his body seemed to wander, at a loss, drifting through his clothes.

But his face was full now, he was pin-neat again, and it had been a good many months since our brother was last awakened in the middle of night, just after his night shift at the bakery, by our mother's whispered apologies. Lost in a thick sleep, free of the bakery's heat, its nausea of sugar, his skinny legs poking out from sheets half-tossed to the floor, Eddy mumbles, Go away. Our mother was always the first to be awakened by the one phone call from the Ninth Precinct they always allowed him. Please, he can't stay there, she tells Eddy, and strokes his head awake. It was a brawl, a turned-over bar stool, a boisterous passing out, another harmless good time Saturday night, unusually cold or rainy, and Eddy would bump shut-eyed down the length of the hall and trudge out into the weather, in the small remaining hours, toward Dad, cursing the cold and shaking his head, ready to offer one last lecture.

In spite of the fact we had not lived with our father for a good dozen years, we were still the one call home, as we would be the only destination for the three suitcases containing evidence of a life that seemed almost illegal, overlooked, left behind in a hurry: his clothes, a single-burner hot plate, a coffee pot spotted with grime, a stack of Five & Dime poses of his sister Helen, a tiny plastic case of photographs, a box of tie pins, a set of Kodaks, spiral bound in bright yellow, of other children we do not recognize, of women we had never met, a driver's license with his own signature misspelled and electric.

Our memory is improvisation, capable of yield, but hazardous and crisscrossed, a collision of tiny pieces. And what we can fashion is not a man but an accident, bits of colored cloth, objects from a bureau top, gaudy and sorry, pleasing and warm, and wrong, put together slapdash with MGM musicals and our mother's stories: a father from the tatters of Sinatra and Astaire when they were new and thin and narrowed down to grace, all cheekbones and jaw, or from the streets, a stranger's gait, the too-sure stride or the slow lost feet, their crumpled speed.

In a dimlit place, any of these things could be true.

But his death is exactly itself. Our father fell over in the street at a weekend's start in December of 1968 and died there of a stroke. It seems at times to be the only thing we know that is a fact. One day, we just believe in it more than anything, though sometimes still expecting, just a little, to see him again, striding too fast and too sure down an uncertain hallway.

Our memory, especially the part that belongs to Louise, lacks a great deal. The landscape is missing. In the trimmed photographs, the children are lifted from the entirety of beaten-down pots and raised voices, and held to a single moment that is true enough but lacking in context, the scissors' edge traveling close to their haircuts and the skin of their arms, lopping off neighbors and their houses, the extent of dusty ground.

Looking down now over Franklin Way, we have this feeling of vertigo, the vertigo of childhood, where the ground escapes at great speed, the vertigo of returning to a place that does not exist, where conversations take place in the past or before we were born. What we used to know—the cattail sway of pleated trousers, a swing set, a pair of striped overalls—seems sprung from the head of Zeus. Midair and there are no solids. Remembering is not the land of things, only a land of great wind where the dead, that never seem to hit the ground, are falling.

It is as if we are driving by, burning up the road, and at the side of our eye, gathering father, pieces that, once assembled, like all of remembered life, fail. A memory is always poorly made. Only the act of memory, the feeling of hurtling headlong, the drive of it, the speed, its grief of completion, is any match for truth. What we retrieve is something vanishing. And what we are left with is an invention which cannot conjure him or replace one single conversation with the living, ecstatic in summer.

Hers

Louise

⌂ In the future, our vertigo ended, and a ground ⌂ came under our feet. Story was a form of gravity.

Memory was the work of the house, and I was telling stories, saying *laundry, buckeye, nettle,* on a morning back home in June.

On my trips to Pittsburgh, I often arrive to rain or its promise along Route 28. From the windows of the New Kensington bus, buckeye, oak, and nettle trees along the brick-paved streets and along the highways blend; it is all the same green history. In summer, always this faint coming of rain, and the presence of my father, who is most clear to me then in the moment before rain. I can see him sitting on his bed in a third-floor room with no books or extra cash, with somewhere to be by 7:00. And from the sidewalks rise the recitations of children, irreplaceable ones, replaced in the streets. And still the women, hopeful and running late, hang laundry over fire escapes, in the strung yards, against the sky in the heat of a summer evening. Mint-green towels, thick with water.

The Natalis' old house in Shadyside is up for sale; the lot sits there silent; only fireflies manage to glitter up the grass. And ours, burnt down long ago and rebuilt into townhouses, is no longer recognizable, except for what I hear in trees and grass.

All that's left is the upward slope of my grandfather's vegetable garden out back and what may be peach, pine, and apple trees, once sticks now thickened into green, and towering. Memory is a laying-on of voices to what has none, as much as it is a gathering from a generous and patient place that will make a gift of its own clear speech. The house at 713 Dorothy Avenue in Shadyside, east side of Pittsburgh, between Elwood Street and Rosary Way is gone, its downward slope of lawn out front flattened to cement, its lot divided into two; two houses, two yards. On every side of this vanished thing, for block after block of the same dark glossy sidewalks, the neighborhood remains. The calm of twenty years ago still seeps from deep within houses, from shady living rooms thick with the blue of TV light, into the greened streets. The houses are changed somewhat with aluminum siding, metal rails, or rambling decks, but stolid, persistent, they sit satisfied with sagging porches, achieved, allowed, handed down to eldest sons or sold in a windfall of real estate.

189

Full grown and towering. Are these the children's trees? Mrs. Guntherman at eighty-three is hanging laundry across the way. In her housedress, hurried by my face, she steps barefoot, ashamed, picking through the grass, through planks of wood, oil spills on the drive. She is shamed by the laundry on the line. I still have your mother's wringer washer, she calls out across the yard, I'm still hanging laundry like a regular hooligan.

Irritable, historical, kind, she leans across the Cyclone fence and peers into my face, Why are you so skinny? Don't they feed you in New York City? Why I just said your name last week; you're a lovely girl, too skinny though; how's your brother? He was such a rip, an ornery cuss; he was my favorite. He has four kids; your sister's got three; and you're not married. Am I right? And your mother, where is she? Who could know her from the phone book anymore? I hear she changed her name, back to what it was.

Full grown and towering. Are these the children's trees? These trees, Mrs. Guntherman. I realize they are all I want to hear about, not one neighborhood sorrow of death at an early age or alone at eighty, felled to the living room floor, not one word of the changes in ownership, the legend of a daughter's career in Guatemala, not news of death or of what else achieved, exchanged over rusty fences, as my own scandal, a love of women, a love of Franny, might be; just trees, their origins and survival.

1955, she says, your mother and you three kids planted that apple in 1955. The peach, she says, pointing to her own yard, we tore that down years ago. And that's

190

another apple now, makes real good yellows, she says, pointing to the peach tree in our yard.

Are these the children's trees? The trunks of peach, pine and apple have divided perfectly into three strong limbs each before the green begins. I take this as a sign, a message grown from the earth, a division of three, because of our love, as if the earth had listened, and responded in trees.

Are these those skinny hopes laid horizontal at my mother's heels, her foot firm and determined, set on the sharp edge of the spade? Whoever plants a tree knows pity, knows how to laugh in the shade, or will learn to someday. Peach, pine, then apple tree. I remember them planted in a different order of green, the pine to the far side and of a different sort, not this wild feathered grace untethered at the center, but needled sharp and contained, and apples not yellow, but green.

A wind-brought green all around us, the yard immense with high tipped-over grass. And when the wind turns circular as Mrs. Guntherman talks, the fate of neighbors is swirling through the trees, and I am brought back to it, to that wind, to its calling through the yard, to its something brewing, all awhirl with what we would become.

Mornings before school, when we had to abandon the yard to its own spread-out day, when leaving it was a lesson in trust that earth, like childhood or our mother, would survive the tight order and fast clip of the day, I learned there was something larger, more constant than our rushed feet, the grip of yellow pencils in our hands,

our bent-down heads. There was a yard with wind in it,
what I knew of eternal space, a wide and yielding em-
brace of grass and sky, within which our tiny strewn
motions took place.

Eager for the spirit of the yard, for any evidence of
my mother's company, I made sure to be the first one
home, entirely capable of finding her there transformed
into air with the smell of her morning bath, or changed
into hairbrush, bowls, perfume bottles on a mirrored tray,
or the paper-thin strokes of the broom's straight path
across the walkway. Sunlight in warmer months better
kept the smell of her, though winter with its shut windows
and doors did not do too badly in holding to the house the
recurrent chime of her bath. There was a certain spirit,
seasonless, in the overlarge furniture, a deepening of its
pillows, a darkening of its arms, or in the just-so-ness of
the starched tablecloth crowned with an arrangement of
plastic roses. The colors of the furniture deepened where
she had sat, and the flat arms of the green upholstered
chair felt lukewarm from the morning light she made a
great show of bringing in, drawing wide the drapes.

This is where I sat each afternoon, in the last of the
sun, with Mother not there, where light was the thing to
adore, unburdened and without a bone, like the wind in
the yard. I would cast out nets that never snagged in that
eternal, bodiless space. And when that space became too
long a place or placelessness, I could remember her, as if
the real facts of life were an aside to light, and burrow
down into the promise of her company.

In the evening, she was ours, though she rarely
spoke. Occasionally she sat in the stuffed green chair,

leafing through magazines she never read but once in a while, reading recipes for hearty soups out loud. Eddy, elbows on his knees, sat listening in his hazy sort of way, leaning against her chair, repentant again, and staying close by way of apology. I lay watching in my hazy sort of way the crisscross of elbows and ankles from under the coffee table, or I watched from the window a constellation of houses shimmer down the block. Helen, with kicked feet, lay flat on her stomach, drawing spiders on the flyleaves of her books, or demanding new clothes, and threatening to tell the truth, that there was something wrong; that our mother was sad, that our father was an unhappy man. This isn't the legacy I wanted to give you, our mother would tell us years later, It had something to do with joy.

The evenings. Occasionally she sat, though usually she ironed and seemed to belong more to our clothes and our hunger for supper than to us. That our father was not there never occurred to me. She bore the weight of all absence. His was long ago poured into her. She was the center, our sorrow defined, and no matter how vague or disallowed our sorrow may have been, she made it manifest in her thinness, in her absence, in her marvelous bowed-down, upright effort on our behalf, and it did not escape us: in one breath, we were solitary and we were hers.

We were hers but she was not ours. She did not belong to us, but to the complicated wheel of raising us, and further, further back, to herself, in a past where we did not exist, a past that made a sharp turn and left itself behind.

193

And we who were scattered somewhere below her far-seeing eye would call to her, and she who was called upon by earthly voices would tilt her head and listen hard to some far-off calling, her ear bent on a destiny, as if she were being summoned to complete a great labor, to sort and to pluck, to gather, to make safe and to reap a turning out of our lives on earth, when really it was only a lost shoe, a nicked finger, our voices confused with some great summons. She would answer then with our interchangeable names, or with Dear God, what is it now? What's happened?

We were the particular slant of her eye turned downward, and we needed forgiveness for our smallness, our grave desire to be touched, for our very predicament of being children, just as she was in need of our forgiveness for her own predicament of being a mother. What wild perfection we had in mind, down to the color of her lipstick.

She knew us in our plainness, our ears exposed, our skin stained with grass. Or she flitted through rooms, and we blurred at the side of her eye. We were round and wondered at, marvelous, we were leaping, we were skin, we were wooden, we were soldiers, nettles, and lovers, distractions from her sorrow, the arrows to its center. We were growing older, rising to the surface, and demanding explanations. We were daughters and son. We were taken here and there. We were refusing to go. Your father, she would tell us years later, he wasn't always well.

Love was sorrow, it was suffering. It giggled only a moment. Its heart was to the wheel, casting out its nets, never pulling them in, fast at rescue, rarely with a moment of its own. It would not let go, admit its greener nature. It was busy, it was urgent, defined by necessity and filled with fast purpose. Heave, she said, and we carted stones to build a patio, freed the walkways from snow. We climbed to the porch roof, painted the gutters while she said a Rosary and clung to the legs of our pants. She stood on window ledges and we clung to her ankles. We were in danger; we were keeping house, lost at top speed on the thin ice of its order. She was following instructions from the Book of the Saints, from the Book of the Mothers, and it was impossible to catch up to her renderings.

But in the morning there could be a moment, in the yard perhaps, when we were still, when we were purely ourselves, recognized by the earth, by the feel of our feet walking across it or standing firm at rest and hidden in its grass, when there was no longer just one of us under a tree, where she stood apart and bothered by the unraveling skeins of existence in the too-quick day, but there were four of us, steered toward each other, toward that moment of becoming a family, a mystery, in a settling down of all things to their nature, unstraightened, or to their true extremes, the soft within the narrow.

She stands in the yard on an early Tuesday morning. We have noticed her from the window, in her gray pedal pushers, in her white cardigan sweater, in a scarf that hides the loose waves of her hair. The peach tree behind her is dappled yellow and white. Although we will go on with our day, unsurprised at her presence, there is something new and unfamiliar about her like the blossoms.

195

Because of the blossoms we have come to the yard and called to her.

We stand there, devoted with the Brownie camera, waiting for just the right moment when she will look at us and her look will gather and release us into some final knowledge of her and of ourselves: we are waiting for that rare moment when she smiles. But the camera chooses her, we choose her, and she is squinting at us, as if wondering our names, her head tilted at the start of a word.

She has been waiting there, squinting at us, all these years, immovable, pondered, wrapped in our sight, in a row of peach, pine and apple trees. We press the button on the Brownie camera, fascinated by the white falls of her sweater against the backdrop of earth, its dug garden, reassured by the bunched sleeves, bothered by the thinness beneath the folds. In love with the full brown curves of hair that frame her face and sweep clear of her forehead, we have asked her to take off the scarf, but the scarf remains and she is squinting at us in sunlight, shielding her eyes, beginning to speak.

On mornings back home in June, with the plain and straight of factory stacks now mainly silent of smoke, with rooftops in slated bunches dreaming themselves into existence along the sides of hills dreamt also, Allegheny River mist rises up from highways along black tracks. My city becomes more and more mirage, its people and the way fog curls slip away from me, nearer to themselves. Then suddenly the straight of bumpy sidewalks, and it is a town of solids again, in flight so constant

196

that it holds. Like some old workings, fine and tuned and made by hand: a clock, a piano, a story, a town. Pittsburgh, Pennsylvania is as solid as an apple and at its core is this: a gray frame house in rain, no longer burning.

What vanishes appears in a flying second, and as I ride along on a crowded New Kensington bus, aware of the sure outline of my own body, angular and singular, I think we could have been created, nearer to the truth, of some lesser cloudy stuff, with the ability of rivers or drafts in an old house. It's no wonder that dance exists, orchestras, or storytelling, where we are asked not to end so sure in outline, but to imagine, to be of this one motion, of which everything is made.

Confusing what I never knew with what I did, all through the city on a visit home in June, I am crisscrossing space, confusing one year with another, a single moment with a myth, or strangers with neighbors, wishing them all endlessly well, as if the heart were smoke, capable of everywhere.

And so I'm in the neighborhood, with childhood in tow, somehow I had it memorized or it memorized me, how I traipsed through it doing chores or disobeying them, making a legend of valentines from paper doilies. And when I spoke, it was usually of the view or something needing to be done. Later on, I wanted to know a story, to be blessed by a single phrase that no one escapes, ambitious toward some necessary geometry of self-placement and inclusion, for these are the same.

Emerging then from this shady place, from this great stirring as through the trees, emerging from the yards, onto the sidewalks, into the stirring as through a mind, something kept flutters down around me, something tiny and common calling from the houses of the neighborhood or along the narrow sides, which may be pigeons from the eaves, which may be a girl, the clatter of knickknacks, a kicked nettle, a skittering thing, till all of sound was like a dwelling; I listened, and for a moment, along with the others, I lived here, in this house.